Of Illustrious Men

Also by JEAN ROUAUD

Fields of Glory

Of Illustrious Men

A Novel by Jean Rouaud

Translated from the
French by
Barbara Wright

ARCADE PUBLISHING • New York

FIRST NORTH AMERICAN EDITION

This is a work of fiction. Names, characters, places, and incidents are either the
product of the author's imagination or used fictitiously.

Library of Congress Cataloging-in-Publication Data
Rouaud, Jean.
    [Des hommes illustres. English]
    Of illustrious men / by Jean Rouaud ; translated from the French
by Barbara Wright.
        p.   cm.
    ISBN 1-55970-265-6
    1. Fathers and sons — France — Loire River Valley — Fiction.
    2. Loire River Valley (France) — Fiction.   3. Death — Fiction.
    I. Wright, Barbara, 1935–   .   II. Title.
PQ2678.07677D4713   1994
843'.914 — dc20   94-13979

Published in the United States by Arcade Publishing, Inc., New York
Distributed by Little, Brown and Company

10   9   8   7   6   5   4   3   2   1

BP

Designed by API

PRINTED IN THE UNITED STATES OF AMERICA

*I*N THE MIDDLE OF THE afternoon he had climbed up on the corrugated iron roof of the shed where the clothes are dried to saw off the branches of the plum tree that had become entangled in the telephone wires after a winter storm. This was a wise precaution. The next strong wind might well bring the whole thing down, temporarily cutting us off from the outside world. Not that Random was situated in an out-of-the-way valley far removed from civilization, but thanks to our telephone we belonged to a sort of caste, a sort of local aristocracy. The country people, who didn't yet possess phones and were reluctant to let the operator know the name of the person they were calling, had gotten into the habit of coming and phoning from our house rather than from the post office, giving us some sort of explanation of the snatches of their conversations, which we didn't even try to overhear but were certainly not going to pass on and distort. We took the greatest care to see that the office door was properly shut and to cover our ears so as not to be like the postmistress. The result was that we felt handicapped by the trust with which we were honored and didn't like to ask people to pay for their calls. But we valued this privilege.

In the winter months, the wind coming in from the Atlantic wasn't satisfied by simply bringing down our telephone wires. It also took the opportunity to deprive us of electricity. How long this lasted varied according to the extent of the damage, and it was sometimes hours before the current came on again. It takes time to mend a cable, to reerect a pole, to repair a transformer. If the house was suddenly plunged into darkness in the evening, we first checked that it was not simply our meter that was at fault. All we had to do was half open the door to the shop and glance through the big window. A streetlight attached to the house at roof level usually cast a cone of filtered light into the shadows. But if the power outage affected the whole district, all we saw was a black hole. Even when the village was enveloped in darkness, though, we could just make out the massive silhouette of the tall houses surrounding the square, and the more imposing one of the church. It looked like a ghost town, like London during the blitz, and we found ourselves trembling. We remembered hearing about the air raids over Nantes during the Second World War, when with all the lights doused the people had to play dead.

Every so often a car would appear at the brow of the hill leading down to the square, its headlights picking up the storm-tossed tops of the three Lombardy poplars planted in a triangle around the town pump, and then it would begin its rapid descent, for a fraction of a second lighting up the bottle of Saint-Raphaël painted on the gable of the *café-tabac*, before disappearing around the corner and once again plunging the town into gloomy silence. No one was more courageous than the solitary cyclist climbing up the hill in the teeth of the wind, swaying from side to side, zigzagging, the slender pencil of his headlight sweeping the road in front of him, its beam just penetrating the inky void, the red light on his rear mudguard still for a long time as he scaled the slope, then stopped, leaned over slightly, and continued at the pace of a pedestrian, pushing his bike by the handlebars. The reflectors on new models had recently become rectangular, and even in the dark this alone enabled us to put the rider down as one of the well-to-do. In local terms, of course, because the only people who treated themselves to new bicycles were those who would never have a car, being either too old, or women, few of whom were adventurous enough to face the derision incurred in aspiring to a driver's license.

Sometimes, too, a faint light piercing the darkness could be seen coming from old Maryvonne's window over her grocery store. As she had a habit of falling asleep over a book — and "wasting electricity" while she was asleep ran counter to her sense of economy — she had devised a method of getting her light from bits of candle, which she chopped up so that the wick went out of its own accord at the very moment she reckoned she would be able to read no longer. She could then drop off with an easy mind, glasses on her nose, nice and comfortable on her pillows, the book falling from her hands. She even claimed that sometimes, at dawn, she would continue her reading in the middle of a phrase, as if her sleep had lasted only for the twinkling of an eye. This scared all the neighbors, who imagined her burning to death, and them with her, and the whole district going up in a gigantic auto-da-fé. They tried hard to dissuade her: she was risking her life, she was ruining her eyes, she had to pay for the rent of her meter anyway, so the game wasn't worth the candle. But quick as a flash the crafty Maryvonne retorted, "And who's going to pay for the electricity I use?" As there were no volunteers, this gave weight to her argument. All the more so since her ancient method of lighting had the merit of costing very little. Given that she was in charge of the upkeep of the church, she was suspected of salvaging the bits of candle that remained stuck on the spikes with their wicks covered in melted wax.

On the day after a long power outage, she would peer over her glasses and pretend to be amazed. Oh, really? She hadn't noticed a thing. The little Voltairean smile at the corner of her lips was her way of getting her pride back after all the disagreeable remarks made about her. And to press the point: "In the old days" — which were still hers to some extent — "we didn't have that kind of problem."

Nor did we. We had oil lamps. When we were quite sure that the whole village was in the same boat, we got them out of the cupboard under the stairs, taking a thousand precautions to keep the fragile glass cylinders upright so as not to risk spilling a single drop of the liquid on the lamp bases, where it would fill the house with its pungent stench. Mother never put the lamps away without carefully cleaning them and wrapping them in plastic bags, fastened with rubber bands to preserve them from the dust. The beauty of the lighting depended on their cleanliness.

When the first men domesticated fire, their faces could certainly not have looked more serious than ours. Striking matches to light the way, we escorted the lamps from the corridor to the kitchen until, with one in the middle of the table and the other near the stove, they provided all the feeble light they were capable of. A very gentle light, which projected our enlarged shadows on the walls and bound us closer together, while outside the wind was blowing a gale. Shrouded in this soothing twilight, we sat huddled together around the table, unable to take our eyes off the incandescent ring at the bottom of the glass chimney over the snakelike wick, which was soaking in the bluish reservoir in the shape of a squashed bulb. As if to warm ourselves, we held our hands up to this source of light and, as a way of playing with fire, soon improvised a little shadow theater. In a column titled "Things To Do on Rainy Thursdays," our children's magazines were always giving illustrated explanations of the way to go about it. But however hard we tried, no matter how we twisted our fingers, we never observed any progress from one time to the next. The duck looked just like the dog, the donkey like the rabbit, the elephant had to make do with a dangling forefinger for a trunk, and the camel lost count of its humps. As for the Indian chief, the only human being in our fabulous menagerie, his feathered headdress composed of five outstretched fingers made him look like a pincushion. In the end, we fell back on what we did best: the bird, which simply consisted of crossing your thumbs and clapping your hands to make slowly flapping wings. An indefinable bird, but at least it had the merit of taking flight when we stretched out our arms, like a dove that has just appeared out of a sleeve.

To control the brightness of the light, there was a little copper wheel down by the burner that you turned to regulate the length of the wick. If the wick was too high, the elongated flame became a dark red spindle and a wisp of soot went wafting up to the ceiling, where it traced a blackish circle. Long after the French Electric Company had improved its network and power outages were only a distant memory, the kitchen ceiling still bore the stigmata of these lamp-lit evenings.

But the damage could be more considerable. One night, a forgotten lamp covered the entire shop with a uniform layer of soot. In the morning, there were fine black particles floating in suspension everywhere, as light as a swarm of flies at the edge of a pond, and the closer you got to the lamp the faster they swirled, making the air unbreathable. They filled our noses and throats. We had only to crack open the door for our faces to turn into those of chimney sweeps.

Mother had to cover herself from top to toe and swathe herself in an old overcoat before plunging, booted, gloved, and hooded, into the cloud of ashes and extracting the guilty lamp, which went on belching out its trail of smoke on the pavement for a long time. When the particles had very gradually settled, when we could see, in a manner of speaking, more clearly, Mother admitted that she didn't know which way to turn, and then said that she must be dreaming — although perhaps not. It was a heartbreaking sight: a post-atomic vision, such as those the futurologists predict for us when the conflagrations started by the nuclear bomb will cover the earth in a grayish coating. Of lesser import, but equally efficient. We had just experienced the paraffin bomb. The shelves holding the brightly colored bowls — orange, green, or lemon yellow — and the shelves with the piles of white porcelain, some of the models gold-bordered, the table on which the sets of delicate cut-glass goblets were lined up, the shelves of red-enamel casseroles — everything had now become charcoal gray, as if the whole shop had been plunged into a bath of tar. A monochrome world, which we carried with us under our soles, because despite all our precautions we couldn't help spreading it everywhere. It was useless wiping our feet on the mat a hundred times, nothing could prevent the imprint of our to-ings and fro-ings remaining on the linoleum like so many elaborately choreographed dance steps. And, in spite of it all, we still had to go out to do the shopping. When we got home people would say: You've been to the butcher's, haven't you? Of course. There was nothing magic about guessing that. They only had to follow our footprints.

We didn't know where to begin. So the first haphazard wipe with a sponge was applied to a corner of a shelf, but this only added to our discouragement; the mixture of soot and water turned into mud that spread out under the dishes, became more deeply encrusted in the grooves in the wood, and launched a black mini-tide that trickled down the cupboard doors, outlining a *Carte du Tendre* on which all the branches of the river led to Despair. As for the sponge, after one wipe with each side, it had to be thrown away.

By a stroke of luck it was a Saturday, and Father, who was a salesman, would soon be home after his week on the road. The onlookers who had come to gauge the scale of the calamity, shaking their heads sympathetically, were all of one mind: Don't do anything until Joseph gets back. Joseph will know. Perhaps because of the ordeals life held in store for him, everyone agreed that when it came to adversity he was in a class of his own. Which was true; we were the first to benefit from it. For instance, if the car happened to break down at two in the morning on a deserted country road, it didn't even occur to us to worry. In similar circumstances other people panic, lock the doors, and bed down as best they can on the seats, waiting for dawn and a passing tractor. But we were quite sure that he would find a solution. He would raise the hood of the Peugeot 403, shine his flashlight on the engine, bend over, push his tie over his back, test a few parts, and, with a bit of wire and one of Mother's stockings, concoct an emergency dressing that would enable us to get home safely. He took a legitimate pride in his makeshift repairs and his gift for improvisation. It was his Leonardo da Vinci side — minus the aesthetic sense. This was how he had invented a way of heating the big bedroom overlooking the street, by getting the pipe from the stove in the shop below to run across it. He had gotten the idea after reading an article in *Historia* (like a lot of autodidacts, he was fascinated by history and ancient stones) about the wall heating in a Gallo-Roman villa. The pipe came up through the floor and then, with bends here and attachments there, made its angular way over to the chimney conduit three or four feet above the head of the bed, which obliged us to take great care when we went to bed and got up. Apart from the unpleasantness, just hitting our heads on it was likely to throw the whole fragile tubular edifice out of kilter. There were contemporary sculptures at the time that looked just like it, which still send people into ecstasies, but when Father showed off his ingenious heating system to relations or friends, we felt rather embarrassed.

He arrived in the early afternoon and as usual parked his car in the square by the side entrance to the church in a maneuver that had become impeccable through frequent repetition, since he was already performing it at the age of fourteen behind his father's back. A whole crowd was there to meet him. Pushing and shoving, they escorted him from his car to the shop, anxious to tell him the latest news. His tall figure with the prematurely white hair towered over the circle of the faithful. Their first stop was at the blackened lamp cooling on the pavement. Eager to hear his reaction, they all nevertheless expressed their own opinions, but this was merely a matter of form, since they would agree with whatever he thought. Everyone said that he was "someone," or "a gentleman," or "a fine fellow," but their way of raising their eyebrows, or pursing their lips, testified to a much richer, much more profound inner feeling, and conveyed their respect, admiration, and allegiance far better than the pathetic conventional terms they used in their attempts to define it. He inspired awe.

Some of them, those who hadn't come off best on this occasion, hadn't forgotten how, a few years earlier, he had changed the minds of everyone in the district when public opinion had almost unanimously decided by way of reprisal to boycott the doctor. If the doctor had merely been content to finish off his patients they wouldn't have objected: a mistaken diagnosis, a dangerous drug, an operation that went wrong — nobody's perfect. But what they reproached him for was much more serious for the former Royalist region, which, two centuries earlier, had watched the Republican armies exterminate the last Vendean troops. A free thinker, the doctor had chosen to be true to his principles and send his little boy to the local lay school. There were only five or six unfortunate children in the school, all of whom were vilified by the hordes in the Christian schools and condemned, in the longer term, to perish in the flames of hell. This might well be proof of his intellectual honesty, but it was a preposterous idea, which in a very short time amounted to putting the skids on him professionally, for the sentence had not been long delayed. Nevertheless, the town had taken the precaution of consulting Joseph the Great, whose lack of enthusiasm for this kind of excommunication they feared. Indeed, he immediately called a parents' meeting, and after a tumultuous session during which the apprentice Inquisitors expatiated on the measures to be taken to send the infidel to the stake, he took the floor: "I am infinitely grateful to Dr. Monnier for having saved the lives of my wife and two of my children. I can see no reason why I should change my doctor." The ban was lifted. The next day, the good doctor's waiting room was crowded with patients.

So now, he showed no surprise at the amplitude of the disaster as he cast his eye over the shelves in their mourning garb, confining himself to the semblance of an inspection designed above all to reassure his audience, contenting himself by way of commentary with running a casual finger over a soup tureen, which left the mark of a white comma on the layer of ashes covering its lid. Standing squarely in the middle of the shop, wiping his soiled finger on his handkerchief (Mother restraining herself from criticizing him), he made the unsurprising remark that he could see no other solution than to put everything to rights. As if all of a sudden his talent for invention had come down to the mundane level. We hadn't needed him, to come to the same conclusion. Our expectations had been of a liturgical order: "Speak but one word and my soul will be healed." He had spoken, but we hadn't made the slightest progress along the road to recovery. As a result, some onlookers were emboldened to think that seen in this new light, Joseph the Great's reputation was altogether overrated. There was a place to be taken. They were already aspiring to the succession, starting to make plans, deciding how to proceed, and suggesting that work begin on Monday. "Tt-tt," Joseph cut in, with the way he had of clicking his tongue against his palate, "not Monday." "When, then?" "Now." Joseph the Great had just signaled his return.

He went up to the first floor and put on his faded, old-rose-colored denim trousers, like the ones fishermen wear, his blue-and-gray-checked cotton shirt (his battle dress for really hard labor; when it was just odd jobs, he simply wore a white shirt and tie and rolled up his sleeves); he collected all the buckets, sponges, and dropcloths the house possessed, then addressed himself to the task of clearing out the shop. The putschists, now returned to the ranks, were immediately enrolled, and a long chain was formed. The dishes were taken out into the yard and plunged into several tubs containing successive decoctions. The water had to be changed nonstop; fertilized by the ashes, it got tipped onto the flowering shrubs, so we got one little benefit from our misfortune. But the water was so black that a plate was sometimes left in the bottom of the tub and got smashed on a stone at the foot of a rosebush. Soon the soaked flower beds were begging for mercy. We covered the whole garden with our manure. In the evening, the earth was disguised as a slag heap.

But there was a monumental quantity of crockery: mountains of plates, soup tureens, glasses, saucepans, stewpans, bowls, casseroles, coffee services, fruit goblets, cheese platters, dishes — earthenware, faience, heatproof, stoneware — flat dishes, hollow, round, square, oval dishes, electric or hand-operated coffee grinders, vegetable mills, potato mashers, ladles, skimmers, sieves, the equivalent of the contents of three hundred kitchen cupboards were emptied out into our yard and joined by milk containers with their aluminum measures, flowerpots of all sizes, jardinières, churns, salting tubs, plastic or galvanized basins, bottling jars, rolls of oilcloth in three widths (36 inches, 42 inches, 48 inches), light bulbs, brooms, brushes, one shelf full of hardware, another of cleaning materials, a thousand oddities such as plaster or wooden eggs used as decoys to trick hens into sitting where they are supposed to, not forgetting the wreaths with their imitation pearls and gems, the marble or granite crosses with Christ in bronze or chromium plate, and the artificial flowers that last from one All Saints' Day to the next and thus accompany one's eternal regrets for a longer time. When we steeped those little barometer manikins that change color according to the weather, however hard we rubbed them they remained gray. We decided that this was normal in damp conditions. Someone suggested putting them in the oven to make them turn pink.

The prevailing atmosphere was one of hard labor. The

women took over from one another and sighed, "There'll never be an end to it," or "Soot — there's nothing worse," or, with a touch of humor, "And to think we'll have to start all over again this evening." Then, in the late afternoon, who did we see arriving? Old Maryvonne, her head covered in a little moiré shawl pulled down over her forehead and discreetly knotted under her chin, as if she'd wanted to cross the square incognito for fear of being suspected of returning to the scene of her crime. Because all day long she'd looked as if she were the accused, behind her counter. Where all our caveats had failed to persuade her of the danger her method of lighting posed to the community, this time events pleaded against her. It was the perfect demon-stration: luckily, our disaster was only a warning sign that had cost nothing (not to anyone else, that is), but it had to be regarded as the first flint that would light the spark of the final holocaust to which she was exposing us all. As the hours wore on, the brave Maryvonne had organized her defense, but the subtle distinction she drew between candles and an oil lamp had convinced no one, and she knew it. So, shaken by the force of events, or more probably wanting to come to the aid of the members of her occult club in their distress, she had closed her grocery store early, bundled a pair of overalls and a pair of old leather-thonged wooden clogs into a shopping bag, and, braving the looks of the people who were already interpreting her gesture of soli-darity as a confession of guilt, offered her help to the group of women harnessed to the monstrous crockery.

In the meantime, the men were washing down the shop from ceiling to floor. Joseph the Great was setting the ex-ample, allocating the tasks and announcing the breaks when their arms felt ready to drop. "Don't mind if I do," said the workers when handed a glass of wine, and the satisfaction they displayed after the first gulp was a sign that their throats were dry and the wine well deserved. After ten hours, the first coat of paint had been applied. The walls and shelves were now of an ivory hue, which didn't entirely correspond to the color shown in the sample on the lid of the paint cans, but this was not the fault of the manufacturers. It was an unprecedented mixture. You only had to look at the workmen as they clocked out: their faces were mottled with both cream and black. Mother suggested they might like to have a shower; some accepted, while others were content to plunge their brawny forearms into a basin and soap themselves vigorously. Not vigorously enough, though, judging by the color of the cloths they wiped their hands on as they went on chatting. As a result of this natural dye, Father's white hair had become darker. But this rejuvenating treatment seemed on the contrary to have fatigued him. He admitted to feeling giddy but blamed it on the turpentine fumes, and, putting a hand on the small of his back in a gesture that was beginning to become familiar to us, unobtrusively straightened himself up, trying to hide the pain on his face.

After one last drink — liqueur, coffee, or herbal tea for the women — he thanked the volunteers one by one, neither exaggerating nor swearing that they had saved his life, going out on the pavement with every single one, even lending old Maryvonne a pocket flashlight, as the streetlights in the square had just gone out at midnight.

On Monday, the shop reopened. It was as crowded as it is at Christmas.

He had a passion for ancient stones. Which means that even though it's so very close, he didn't often take us to see the sea. When it comes to antiquity, the sea is unbeatable; it was already there when the world saw its first mornings. But its elusive side, its water lying dormant above chasms, its waves coming and going without really making up their minds, its tides ebbing and then flowing back six hours later to reclaim by stealth the bit of beach they have given you — the sea is nothing like our father. Him we spontaneously classified among things solid. We conjectured that stones, in his eyes, possessed the quality of the estimable man, the man who protects, builds, and doesn't yield. A chaos of rocks, a menhir, or a skillfully bonded wall was like a genealogical tree to him. This monolithic kinship made him feel one of the family. Whereas water flows, forgetful of its source, breaks its word, engulfs, effaces its traces, inundates, oxidates, damages, and water doesn't support anything — unless in a rather hard winter it is the alternating, well-balanced step of a skater on a frozen lake. Perhaps in such conditions he would have preferred an ice floe, that tangible, subdued sea that throughout the ages has imprisoned piles of fossil annals in its strata of accumulated snow, but the last Ice Age was too long ago in the Lower Loire.

All our outings led us toward stones. Castles, of course, but the castles of the Loire, even though none were missing from our agenda, interested us less: too beautiful, too clean, too opulent, too bourgeois — decors for princesses with peas under their mattresses and secret love affairs. And then, the mild weather in Anjou conspires to deal gently with limestone and tufa. For a soft climate, soft stone. Father possessed the kind of austerity that felt more at home with granite. So on the long Easter and Pentecost weekends, he would take us on a guided tour of Brittany. There, the whole substratum resounded with this secret message, rising from the depths: granite is a rock as hard as men are sometimes hard — from having had too many crosses to bear. It is a crystalline rock, magmatic, formed in the entrails of the earth. The pressures on it are so great that the volume of an airy immensity is reduced to the dimensions of a diamond. And what the Armorican substratum has borne is no less than a Himalayan chain.

We were in the primary era, and everything still remained to be done. A powerful folding movement thrust tall islands up out of the depths of the waters. The Armorican Massif was then more than fifteen thousand feet high, a dinosaur before the dinosaurs, tropical before the tropics, because the prevailing climate of these first lands was hot and humid. When people boast of the charms of the past, they always forget this Polynesian phase of Brittany. But if you are a painter in Pont-Aven, this could save you the money spent on a fruitless journey to the Tuamotou Archipelago. The entire island was covered by a dense forest, necessarily virgin because no one ever came across either druids, birds, or mammals, not even those tall, clumsy creatures with long necks that weren't giraffes. What caused our Hercynian Mountains to be leveled? The wind, which blows on our coasts; the rain, which our skies lavish on us; and time, with a modicum of infinite patience. On a smaller scale, we can understand it better. Take a few million pilgrims, hang a cockleshell around their necks, send them by any route to Galicia, and ask them, as they enter the triumphal porch of the cathedral, to place a hand on its central column. Come back five centuries later, and the pilgrims' sweat has left a deep impression of five fingers in the granite. A breath of air, provided it doesn't lose heart, is enough to raze mountains. Today, their highest point rises to no more than twelve hundred feet. With a bit more time, with a few more squalls, the Armorican Massif will resemble the plains of Beauce — minus their fertility.

Brittany was his chosen land. He crossed the length and breadth of it six days out of seven, working for a Quimper wholesaler located on the bank of the Odet River in the rue du Vert-Moulin. It wasn't hard to remember the address: rue du *Vermoulu* — "Worm-eaten," he would joke when business was going badly. His area covered the five departments of Brittany, but not the little bit south of the Loire where the estuary, in the days before the bridges spanned it, formed a natural frontier. To organize his itineraries in the best possible way, he had stuck the local Michelin maps of the region on a plywood bulletin board and, by juxtaposing them, reconstituted a greater Brittany, which covered one whole wall of the office. It was pierced by hundreds of map pins with different-colored heads, each color representing one of his clients. He only had to glance at it to know what was what. He had worked out a complicated code, which he alone had mastered, in which the colors referred to the turnover achieved, to the frequency of his visits, to new possibilities for sales, and to other criteria that escaped us. We knew, for instance, that the green heads saw him less often than the red heads, and that the blue heads, either because he expected more from them or simply because it was worth making a detour to call on a friend, enjoyed his special attention. As for the black heads, they were invited to make a bit of effort if they didn't want to disappear from this Breton constellation. And since he had a range of some ten colors at his disposal, he also indicated the pleasant hotels, the good restaurants, and even a few sights, the destinations of our next family outings.

On Sunday evenings he closeted himself in his office, brought his accounts and order books up to date, and wrote the cards stamped with his name that he mailed to his clients to advise them of his next visit. Then, stationing himself in front of his wall chart, which, over the parts showing the sea, he had embellished with photographs of the most beautiful sites in the region, and as if he were planning his strategy on the eve of a battle, he worked out his future routes, joining the colored pins with cotton thread that traced, according to the Euclidean principle of the shortest distance, an ideal geometrical route, a zigzagging aerial view that represented, like a diagram or a temperature chart, his schedule over the next month. Week after week, in broken lines, the threads indicated Ariadne's paths, which furtively thwarted our father the minotaur. The threads too were of different colors and, when weighted at both ends with copper buttons to keep them tight, managed to avoid encroaching on one another. And, while methodically exploring an area, they would sometimes meet at a place where he enjoyed staying the night, thus doing his best to reconcile the clients to be called on with his favorite hotels, sure as he was of chancing upon two or three fellow travelers there and playing a game of cards with them after dinner.

He hesitated for a long time before deciding on the most judicious solution, kept changing his mind — instead of that point in the north, why not try that other one more to the west? — and every time a new variation, an unknown itinerary, depended on these options. When a particular one seemed to lead to an impasse, he untied the thread circulating between the colored heads and started again from zero; that's to say from Quimper, where he arrived every Monday morning, having left Random at six, with nothing inside him by way of breakfast but the smoke from his first Gitane cigarette.

Two hundred kilometers to drive at a stretch was no picnic. Whereas nowadays they do their best to bypass them, in those days the gravelly, narrow, winding roads passed through every little village. The small towns, confined within the perimeter of their ancient ramparts, with their crowded markets and their cramped streets, all constituted obstacles to the progress of the traveler. For that was how salesmen liked to describe themselves. The word didn't evoke any dream of evasion, any image of a far-off country, of golden sands bordered with coconut palms: a traveler was simply someone who earned his living on the road.

The moment you left a main road and penetrated into the labyrinth of the Breton countryside, you had to reckon with the droves of cows blocking the whole width of the road with their disenchanted gait; corpulent, sensual creatures with their udders bouncing about between their hind legs and almost touching the ground, ruminating the same immeasurable ennui between their jaws, as if having to carry that strange geography of brown continents and ivory oceans on their bulging flanks had convinced them they had traveled around the world. The cowherd, male or female, followed on a bicycle, a stationmaster's little red flag tucked under his or her arm with which, should the occasion arise, to direct the traffic, feigning with suitable dignity to hear nothing when the sound of a horn betrayed a driver's impatience, continuing at an unvarying speed, almost losing his balance because he had to ride so slowly, taking in bumps and potholes with the same heavy pressure on the pedals, only dismounting at the bottom of the steepest slopes, and always at the same place, getting back on his bike at another landmark — that tree, for instance, which indicated the spot where the slope became gentler. Such is the routine, along the road ritually followed morning and evening, of this twice-daily transhumance. Could the pasture be brought closer to the farm by an exchange with a neighbor? The cowherds sometimes think about it, but immediately reject the idea of asking a favor — how humiliating — and anyway that would upset the established pendular movement in the wake of the indolent beasts, that is, upset the motion of the planets, the beautiful alternation of days and nights, the cycle of the seasons in accordance with which life, however wretched, has so far been organized, and will still be organized tomorrow. Any change, even if it were conducive to greater comfort, would certainly bring with it some hidden disadvantage, and also, if the working of the clock were disrupted, something like death.

The dog, sure of its importance, keeps running up and down fore and aft of the herd, straightens out the recalcitrant or laggardly cows, makes its voice heard to gain respect. From time to time it comes and looks up at its master to claim his approval. He's a gentle, ugly mongrel, who has never known what it is to be patted and who, like most of his dubious breed, is very likely to be called Whitey or maybe Patches — merely because of the white patches on his lower legs. Imagination is not the strong point of country folk, who consider it wiser and more reassuring for things to be repeated identically. It was the Crusaders, on their return from Palestine, who invented the idea of baptizing the faithful animal in the name of those "dogs of infidels," so we still come across a few dogs called Médor. But no one would want to choose their names from the calendar of saints. That would be to blaspheme against the Holy Spirit, the only sin that is not remissible.

As for cats, they have no civil status. In generic terms, they are just "cats" — and it's a mistake to feed them because when their bellies are full they won't even bother to chase mice anymore, which after all is their function, and why we tolerate them. They are saddled with the old tradition of bringers of bad luck, which transforms them into scapegoats and sometimes into quarry, when there's nothing better to kill. It is not unusual to come across their famished corpses riddled with shot in the hollow of a furrow. Some have a more enviable fate and can bask, supremely indifferent, on the rim of a well or groom themselves interminably on a windowsill.

On other occasions it's a horse and cart that enjoins the motorist to take his foot off the accelerator. The man stands on the cart, keeping a loose hold on the reins, as upright as a charioteer. His feet are wide apart, to ensure his balance. This stance is also the assertion of his power — that, for instance, of preventing anyone from passing him. He wears faded blue denim overalls, with patches of a darker indigo sewn over his bottom and his knees, a reminder of his garment's long-forgotten original color. Frequently, with a Napoleonic gesture, he inserts a free hand into the bib of his overalls. But the essential attribute of his caste, his fetish, is his cap, whose peak pulled down over his eyes both protects him from the

setting sun and makes him look like a person of consequence. His cap is more important to him than his horses;
it is only separated from him at bedtime, although it comes
as quite a surprise, when he takes it off for a moment
to scratch his head, to see a pure white tonsure, in
sharp contrast to the coppery red of the back of his neck,
which has been tanned by the sun and the inclement
weather.

When he feels that the car behind him is becoming impatient, he sends a rapid movement rippling down the reins
that smacks the hindquarters of the horse and makes it get a
move on for three paces, but it very soon reverts to its weary
walk. Often, sitting at the back of the cart, her legs dangling, both hands clutching the rails, his wife comes eye to
eye with the motorist facing her behind his windshield, and
she alone has to brave his wrath. In such cases, she becomes
absorbed in the contemplation of a landscape she has seen a
thousand times, and in which there is nothing to be seen,
and contents herself with pulling her autumn-colored
smock down over her thigh when a rut jolts her and dis-
closes a knee as white as her husband's balding head. Her
rubber boots only come up to mid-calf, and so reveal her
thick gray wool socks. She wishes herself a thousand
leagues away and prays to heaven that the road will soon
widen and give the irascible driver room to pass. To keep
her composure, with an exquisite gesture she pushes a lock
of hair back under her scarf. Which gives one to understand
that the art of good manners is found just as naturally in the
country as it is in the town. She is greatly relieved when the
cart finally turns into a side road.

Father's clients did not all own large businesses. In
the impoverished Brittany of the interior, in the isolated

villages, most of the retail outlets were more or less general stores, in comparison with which our shop in Random could be seen as a model of specialization. Was this due to their geographical situation? Entering these glory-holes with their multiple odors, you found yourself back in the days of "the Conquest of the West," when the bazaars that flourished along the railroad offered the new colonists bacon, gunpowder, and lace. As each new demand appeared in the commune, fly papers and pink and green sachets of shampoo would find themselves cheek by jowl on the counter with a long-playing record of a compilation of the most popular operettas, interpreted by the king of the accordion and his great orchestra of three musicians. In this quasi-economy in the mountains, all needs had to be catered for: from bottle gas to writing paper, not forgetting fancy cups and saucers, "a souvenir of my first communion." This is where Father came in.

He would sometimes go dozens of kilometers out of his way just to sell two glasses and three plates to a general store–café in some obscure village in the Arcoat. Brittany had a gift for these heterogeneous shops in which married couples combined their talents as one adds a string to one's bow in the hope of ameliorating the run of the mill. Some were real Jacks-of-all-trades: market gardeners in the morning, hairdressers in the afternoon, and insurance agents in the evening. The bar was their indispensable source of income. Demanding no specific skill from its proprietor except that of succeeding in filling glasses to the brim (with that precise knack of half turning the bottle to prevent the last drop from trickling down its neck), it guaranteed a minimum but constant income, as the consumption of alcohol by the most fervent drinkers never flagged until they were on their deathbeds. Besides, the more bars there were to visit — the only tried and tested remedy against boredom and solitude — the more it delayed the dreaded moment when there was nothing else to do but go home. In Random, a village that, modest as it was, nevertheless boasted no less than seventeen cafés, you could tell the precise time of day by the state of intoxication of their most assiduous habitués. On Sundays, for instance, when Monsieur So-and-So, who progressed with metronomic regularity from one bistro to the next, came staggering up to his last port of call, everyone knew that it was two in the afternoon, that we had just finished our chocolate éclairs, and that Madame So-and-So, his wife, had been waiting stoically since the end of High Mass, her handbag on her knees, in the last remaining car parked in the square.

As for Monsieur René, he was a sundial in himself. And there was no need for the sun to shine for his nose to become red: rutilant, granular, a street-market strawberry. He was a veteran of the first war who was ending his days in the old people's home and who shuffled along leaning on two canes. His entire day was occupied by two great circuits of the square, with a systematic halt at each café. In the interval, he went back to the canteen for his lunch. Considering the speed of his movement in four-four time (one foot, one cane, the other foot, the other cane) and the steep slope joining the old people's home to the village, it could be said of Monsieur René that he was a very busy man.

The ritual of this fatal merry-go-round was immutable. You pushed open a café door, you greeted the assembled company, and the company wouldn't allow you to leave until each of its members had stood everyone a round, which, arithmetically, made as many rounds as there were drinkers, not forgetting one last one for the road. It's not difficult to imagine the risks run by a traveling salesman circulating in a region constituting the five most alcoholic departments in France. However, Joseph must have grown weary of these summit meetings in which business is conducted by clinking glasses, because his signature is to be seen at the bottom of a document in which he signs a pledge that he will never again touch a drop of alcohol. Maybe he had gone over the limit a few days before, but he kept his pledge, and in the middle of a circle of inebriates he would order a peppermint cordial without wavering. No one would ever have had the bright idea of playing the devil's advocate. Pure waste of time.

However meager the eventual order, it would nevertheless have obliged him to show his client the contents of ten or so suitcases crammed into the trunk and the dismantled backseat of the Peugeot 403. Every Saturday, when he got home he emptied the car of its load and replaced the backseat, with a view to a possible Sunday outing with the family. On Sunday evenings he reversed the process. As the car was not designed for such use, he had concocted a flooring of skillfully cut planks that fitted into one another like pieces of a jigsaw puzzle and facilitated the storage of the suitcases. This gantry remained in place when the backseat was reinstalled, the result being to raise it and allow us to see over Father's head when he was driving. On the other hand, he asked us to lower our own heads during a delicate maneuver; owing to our elevated position, we were all he could see in the rearview mirror.

Now, cram into a specially adapted cubic suitcase some fifty plates of different patterns, pick it up, cross the street, push open the shop door, put the thing down, undo the leather strap buckled around it to prevent the whole thing from coming apart, unpack, display, go into your sales patter, put up with the dumb show of the shopkeeper who by this means is from the very beginning preparing his refusal and has no wish that any signs of admiration on his part might cause a misunderstanding. Repack it without a sigh. Pick it up again, go back to square one. Repeat the operation. Bring out that suitcase full of glassware with its compartments lined with red velvet, that other one full of knickknacks (some of which may be chipped) cursorily wrapped in squares of cloth, and then that other one, and then yet another that you'd forgotten but which, knowing your client's taste, you tell him you're quite sure will interest him. Say: I'll be back in a minute. Come back quickly, your arm nearly pulled out of its socket by that quasi-trunk that you almost have to drag over the ground. Never show how weary you are. Explain: top quality, seconds, special offer, introductory offer, recommended price, limited stock. Demonstrate the splendor of that cut-glass item, designed to hold fruit or whatever you like, by flicking its rim with your fingernail to make it ring. Ask about various people. Sympathize. Don't insist. Create a diversion. Forecast the weather, say: It's going to clear up. When your client starts telling you that life is hard for his profession at the moment, counter with: It's the same everywhere. The order book is ready to hand, balanced on a pile of samples, its cover and the pages you've already filled folded back. Slip a couple of pieces of carbon paper under the original so as to make two more copies: one for the Quimper wholesaler, another for the retailer, and the third for you. Bring out your ballpoint pen, which you appreciate because it doesn't leak in your pocket like a fountain pen, and write down, being careful to put everything in its proper column: item code, description of article, item price, quantity (you'll do the numbers tonight at your hotel). Say: I'm listening. Two of this model, one of that one, and three of this sort. Will that ditches strewn with violets and pink pansies; the wheat fields dotted with poppies and cornflowers, thus combining the promise of bread with a "Say it with flowers" — a jumble of plant life that constituted delicate shrines of verdure around the sacred fountains, those open-air fonts that preserve, in a pious trickle of water, the miraculous memory of a hermit saint whose probable inexistence was in no way prejudicial to his certified healing virtues. For the heavens that were so miserly with the sun were prodigal of these gifts. This was proved by the little granite chapels scattered around the countryside like so many prayers sent up into the four winds. All that was needed for one to be built was for a member of the lesser nobility to have had a prayer granted, or a laborer's ploughshare to bump into a statue of the Virgin that some mysterious hand had buried in the subsoil, like an egg on Easter morning. Once the miracle had been confirmed, each chapel adopted its own indulgence, the specialty of these devout folk who liked to dress up in their Sunday best and go on pilgrimages behind a forest of gorgeously embroidered banners, chanting songs of praise to the greater glory of their patron saint and Saint Anne, who, by a few judicious apparitions (what's the use of appearing to the village idiot? who would believe him?) had let it be known to the Bretons that she had placed their region under her very special protection — a wink in the direction of the oldest Daughter of the Church (France) who had chosen her daughter (the Virgin Mary) without even obtaining the Virgin's consent. These pilgrimages not only earned indulgences, they also provided an occasion to look up long-lost distant cousins who lived about eight kilometers away and to spot the marriageable girls whose native parishes could be identified by the subtle variations in their lace coifs. The processions wound their way through the labyrinthine landscape, the gold crosses and the songs of the faithful rising above the hedges, a land in such perfect harmony with the tortuous progress of its people's souls that the indulgences disappeared with it in the great cataclysm that, in the early sixties, deliberately hastened the slow process of erosion as if, following the demolition of the confessional, the sinners had given up going to confession.

For there is a before and an after in Brittany: the before of the tiny little landholdings, the headache of the land-registry experts, which in the case of a large family got parceled out until the heirs were left with just enough land to stand up on and the right to emigrate, and the after of the regrouping when, in view of the pathetic yields produced by Breton agriculture, the top-level decision was taken to force the whole region to come to terms with modernity. Modernity is recognized by the fact that it refuses to make do with the leftovers. In those shrunken fields, how could anyone operate those enormous machines that in a single hour can get through a week's work for ten men? How can the earth be fertilized without the nitrogen dressing that encourages the growth of bindweed and daisies? How can the starlings be prevented from pecking at the sown grain, and thus devouring the anticipated harvest? How can the peasant be induced to abandon his barren soil by extolling the merits of the life of the factory worker and the delights of the city? How can what is now dispersed — fields, houses, animals — be integrated? How can what is now integrated — generations, memories — be dispersed? The great Creator-Designer, closeted in his study, swept a devastating arm over Brittany the way a drunken soldier clears a cluttered table. Having removed its blemishes, he redrew the land in vast rectangles; he drew nice wide straight tracks over it, and then, seeing that it was good, he appended his signature to his great creation. The *lettre de cachet* was sent to this distant province, and the work of devastation could begin.

It was explained to the peasant, who was used to shuttling back and forth behind his animals, that from now on he would be able to keep an eye on them from his window. By what miracle? His few scattered acres were going to be turned into a single, continuous tract of land adjacent to his farm. The negotiator, who was expecting to see a grateful smile spread over the man's face, very soon came to the conclusion that these people were never satisfied. But would this reconstituted land yield as much as the bit down by the river? A little less, but that was why he was being offered a few extra acres in compensation. In other words, more land to cultivate, and more work, for produce of inferior quality. How did that even things up? And in such an exchange, who would inherit that good bit of pasture down by the water? The fellow who has been coveting it and who's on such good terms with the authorities? At this stage of the negotiations, the representative of the Republic realized he had no alternative but to retreat.

The discussions fostered resentments, revived old quarrels. Supporters and adversaries of the regrouping opposed one another vigorously. The cafés became the echo of these stormy debates. The tiniest bistro was transformed into a revolutionary Procopius. The whole thing was beginning to look like a new Dreyfus affair, dividing families and communes. Rumors spread: about one man who'd seen the value of his land multiply tenfold since he'd managed to get them to run a road through it; about another who'd been cheated and had decided to put an end to it all. No one knew exactly how, but the regrouping was fraught with menace. Some of them threatened to stop the invaders by chaining themselves to their fences. There was no counting the number of people who declared it would only happen "over my dead body." But without waiting for the outcome of these discussions, the bulldozers went to work.

All day long the drone of their engines could be heard throughout the countryside, sometimes getting louder when they came up against an unexpected obstacle, perhaps a recalcitrant tree stump, increasing in intensity, infuriated that anything should oppose their progress. When they stopped for a break, you needed a moment's silence before you could feel you were once more at home in space, as if it had been blown to smithereens and was cautiously resettling itself. Your ear had become so accustomed to the racket that at first it found the absence of noise strange, but it gradually reeducated itself by enjoying the song of a bird, the sound of the wind, the rustling of the leaves, or the passing squelch of a moped going by in the rain.

The gigantic mechanical diggers cleared the way for new roads just as the fancy took them. You could easily see where the roads were being planned by following the zip-lines of their caterpillar tracks. They shaved off the hedges without even seeming to notice them, crushed the brushwood with contempt, bashed into the hedges as you might kick aside an anthill, filled in the ditches and horse ponds, laminated the mounds on which the cows liked to station themselves to enjoy a better view of the landscape.

Even the great haughty oak trees were subjected to the

law of the strongest. The front blade of the bulldozer
wedged itself against the bark, the engine revved up at full
throttle, and the enormous mass began to push. In vain.
The trunk remained motionless, confident of its legend,
displaying an obstinate assurance. But then the fury of the
machine was communicated to the whole earth. The vibra-
tion of the levers, those vertical metal shafts crowned with a
black Bakelite knob, sent a tremor through the entire body
of the man clutching the controls. The caterpillar tracks
started skidding. Faced with this energy run riot, the
branches began to sway. You hoped it was all just an optical
illusion caused by the clouds drifting by behind the foliage,
the way the moon seems to glide through the storm clouds.
But on this presumption, the machine merely increased its
violence, an enraged ram intent on the destruction of its
victim, and the facts soon had to be faced: the clouds were
indeed passing by, but the tree was inclining. It didn't come
crashing down, like a tree yielding to the axe. With each
degree of inclination it clung on with all its might, refusing
to capitulate, but when at last its roots were laid bare they
had at least taken with them a chunk of Mother Earth as
proof of their evisceration. After one last triumphant
thrust, the tree was finally flattened in a rustle of foliage
drowned by the sound of the engine, and it lay with its
branches and roots on either side of its bole, like a symmet-
rical bone.

In the middle of an orchard, it was an unequal contest.
Despite their numerical superiority, the old apple trees
drawn up in battle order soon regretted having teased the
valiant warrior in the yellow armor. The machine pivoted on
its axis, trying to breach the circle of its assailants — on your
right, Sire, on your left — and the tortured trunks went
flying like straws in the wind. No more apple trees, no more

apples, no more cider, no more home distillers. It was said that the drivers got a bonus for every tree they felled. We imagined them drawing little miniature forests on their monsters' flanks, like the marks fighter pilots make on the fuselage to show the number of planes they have shot down.

Nothing seemed to be able to stop them, these methodical hordes who were carrying out a new kind of scorched earth policy in the name of reason. Uniformly sweeping away everything in their path, one by one they stripped mysterious Brittany of her veils, allowing the eye, amazed to be able to reach so far without any intervening curtain of trees, to see the land of Arcoat as naked as the faces of Persian women when Pahlavi's soldiers forcibly unveiled them. The residue of this great earthwork was piled up at the far end of the plain, the way a housewife temporarily deposits a little heap of dust on her doorstep; gigantic, sepulchral accumulations of earth and brushwood with which the passing years gave asylum to the new landscape's rejects: self-propagating weeds, bramble bushes, gorses, and homeless birds, allowed to build their exhausted colonies in these primitive encampments. The progressive cleansing of a rebellious community. The work of annexation, begun in the bed of the little lame duchess, Anne of Brittany, in which two kings of France slept, was complete.

Usually, it's only war that can redefine a landscape so violently. History does indeed record a war during those years, but it was on the other side of the Mediterranean, and it was only its faint echo that reached us. Or was it a shock wave, caused by the last world cataclysm and arriving twenty years later? Or again, triggered by our century, which has accustomed us to perform acts of destruction,

It was during these days of disaster that the traveler kept watching the number of kilometers mounting up on the odometer. For quite some time he had been preparing himself to cross the line of a hundred thousand, a symbolic equator both for the car and for its driver, who had just traveled, in no more than two years, with neither accident nor major breakdown, the equivalent of two and a half times the circumference of Earth. These were somewhat unusual circumvolutions, though, as they were wound, like a ball of wool, around a tiny little territory, as if Magellan had gone in for coastal fishing and, though having spent the same number of days at sea, instead of in the famous Strait, had merely offered the world a modest portolano describing places he had already visited a thousand times. To get a better idea of the prowess of the Peugeot 403, you had to measure it against the performance of its predecessors. The blue-gray Renault Juvaquatre, which dated from the period immediately following the war and therefore had limited resources, had been valiant — a sort of packing case on wheels bought, in those days of shortages, without tires, which were later acquired by bartering ration coupons and American army tank crews' goggles. But since it held the road as if it were running on cakes of soap, it would have had great difficulty in tackling, like its successor — a black and chrome Peugeot 203 van — the tortuous reliefs of the Massif Central, the roads in the Limousin in which the grass pushed its way up through the cracks in the pavement, or the high Pyrenean passes in the days when Father was traveling on a circuit as vast as half of France, including the

French-speaking part of Belgium, canvassing primary schools in an attempt to sell educational wall charts, a series on various themes illustrated with ten plates: Anatomy (with a cutaway diagram of a body strangely lacking in genitals), Natural Science, Great Discoveries (from a hairy man scraping away at a flint on top of a little pile of dead leaves to Pasteur observing rabies at the bottom of a test tube), Geography (two series: France and The World), History (the whole of Michelet in ten plates: Vercingétorix with his mustache in the shape of Napoleon's cocked hat, Clovis and his baptism, Saint Louis washing people's feet between crusades, Jeanne d'Arc and her fringe, Jeanne Hachette looking like a pale imitation of the earlier Jeanne, Louis XI and his little hat drawn in section like a flying wing, Sully and his two breasts, Louis XIV posing as a fashionable fencer, the Battle of Fontenoy and its courteous dead, the Bastille and its storming, Bonaparte and his Bridge of Arcola, the Duke of Aumale and Abd-el-Kader's retinue, Gambetta and his hot-air balloon), not forgetting the biblical series, especially produced for Christian schools with the aim of capturing a new market but which, despite an extremely modest Eve veiled by her hair à la Lady Godiva, didn't sell, because right-minded clients suspected the publishers of having Communist sympathies (some of them had even seen a resemblance to Marx in the bearded, long-haired portrait of Moses brandishing the Tablets of the Law, and claimed that instead of the Ten Commandments they represented the dogmas of dialectical materialism, and instead of Israel, the promised land of the Soviets). This was how the publisher of the educational charts went bankrupt, and why we still had dozens of reproductions of our red Moses in the garden shed. Father had even papered his workshop with them. An occasional carpenter, our Joseph did his odd jobs surrounded by his refuseniks.

Why did he need to travel so far for such poor returns? He was away for weeks on end, sending us a postcard from every town he stayed in. We made a collection of them, which constitutes an erratic itinerary and at the same time a kind of pointillist log book — San Sebastián and its long sandy beach: "Shoes aren't any cheaper in Spain, and it's raining"; Amiens and its cultivated marshlands (a flat-bottomed boat on a canal bordered with reeds): "For my great big father who likes boats so much" (what sort of a father is this, who calls his son his father?); Reims and its smiling angel to his younger daughter, who is so very lively: "The angel is pleased, a little bird told him to tell me that you are very sweet"; the Millevaches (or "Thousand Cows") plateau, to his big seven-year-old daughter: "Now that you can count up to a thousand, how many cows are there on this plateau?" (we turned the card every which way, but we couldn't find a single cow either in the trees or in the clouds); two cards from Brussels, one of the Grand' Place, the other of the Manneken-Pis, that impudent little fellow twenty inches tall, stark naked, urinating from his pedestal into the basin of a fountain: "Don't copy him"; Rodez, a panoramic view of the town in Ektachrome, in which he talks about money, of how much he has promised himself he will earn (he won't come home until he has reached the target he has set himself), of the money order he's sending us, part of which is to be spent on repaying Monsieur X and the rest on paying the two outstanding bills in his desk drawer. This is the postcard on which in his delicate, individual handwriting he confesses how much he misses his family; it is clear how very weary he is, he

sends all his love to his wife and three children, and it is
obvious that he is working himself to death, that he de-
serves a far better life than the one fate had had in store for
him, and that he had probably not managed to work out the
proper way to lead such a life; — it was as if he were mainly
spending his time in spending his time.

He had adapted the back of the 203 so that the charts
could be stored vertically and would slide effortlessly along
rails ingeniously fixed top and bottom. In fact, that was
what fascinated him — the possibility of using any sort of
situation to put his powers of invention to the test.

Perhaps he had even accepted the job in order to have to
solve the problem of storing the charts. And once he'd
sorted that one out, there was nothing to do but go looking
elsewhere, around Quimper way, where another problem
arose: how to stow suitcases of different sizes, not in a van
anymore (the 203, having had its day, was sold to a builder,
who got a bargain when you consider that twenty years
later it was still to be seen driving through the streets of
Random) but in an elegant four-door sedan, a brand-new
model that unlike its predecessor didn't make you think of
work.

Halfway through the "Trente Glorieuses," now that
things were looking up after the necessities had been provided for, we were able to make concessions to aesthetics.
And they were big concessions. With its flowing and rather
soft lines, all its angles systematically rounded, its ivory-
colored molded plastic dashboard with its red and green
lights, the Panhard Dyna was like a portable transistor
radio. Everything, except the weather, made you feel like
laying a beach towel down beside it — which in any case
would have been useful for looking under its chassis when,
after a few weeks and only very shortly after the breaking-

in period, it began to shed oil and nuts and bolts. But in any case it wasn't in the nature of the Dyna to be silent; its designers probably thought that an engine that could be heard a long way off added a sporting touch, like the young men who disconnect the exhaust pipe of their mopeds, stick their heads down over the handlebars, and keep changing imaginary gears. But as the Dyna went on playing Tom Thumb, it became impossible to carry on a conversation in it, since its assorted noises made the engine's powerful voice the only thing that could be heard. So rather than yell, we concentrated on the landscape. When we were on a journey, the driver would point out the sights without saying a word. We turned our heads to the right: a menhir, a calvary; to the left: a ruined castle, a horse. If his finger pointed upward: an airplane. The explanations came later, when we took a break. So it wasn't an airplane, but a glider. A glider? That's to say an airplane without an engine that is carried in rising currents of hot air. Without an engine? We glided with it in a vertiginous silence.

The suitcases piled into the back had very soon got the better of the suspension. We could have written a guide to the state of the Breton roads in which the milestones would have replaced the stars and the road signs. People who protested in the name of tradition against the paving of the cobbled roads, which were still numerous in the region, should simply have got on board the Dyna. Our teeth never stopped rattling all the way through the ancient towns.

To be honest, it wasn't only his heavy suitcases that were responsible for the state of the shock absorbers. His hobby hadn't helped. It was during this period that he started to collect unusual stones. During the week he spotted them at the side of the road, stopped, took the smallest ones, rolled the bulkier ones into the ditch or hid them behind a tree, and when he got home he marked them on his wall map with brass-headed studs — the only ones to be stuck in the open country. On some Sundays, the whole family set off to retrieve them.

Our postman Cheval had planned an ideal garden that he never had time to make, contenting himself with piling up his booty at the far end of the plot in anticipation of his great building project. Father had made a few pencil sketches featuring rockeries and a waterfall, which evolved every time he made a new discovery. Some of the sketches were more definitive. His rocky chaos, from which a spring would have gushed, was to have been six feet high. Concealed within its mass was a rudimentary but sophisticated device, very much like the heating pipes in the bedroom, which, by extending the gutters on the little garden house where our Aunt Marie lived (actually *his* aunt), would have fed his system with rainwater. Theoretically, in accordance with the principle of communicating vessels, the fountain would have risen to the eaves, but since he was afraid that the reality might prove somewhat rebellious, and even though rain is far from being a rare commodity in the Lower Loire, he had planned a parallel circuit running from the old well, disused since we had been connected to the water main. This circuit would have been used only occasionally, when inquisitive people were visiting, or to welcome friends.

There were two goldfish in a bowl, waiting for the basin at the foot of the rocky chaos that they had been promised. They had been the origin of the whole project. Out of compassion, on account of the exiguity of their abode. But the idea had already been in the air. Now that it was once again possible to make concessions to the superfluous, kitchen gardens and the "fear of going without" were retreating before the invasion of lawns adorned with cherubs, flowered cartwheels, or Snow White's seven pocket-sized companions captured in their principal activity, which consisted of pushing a child's wheelbarrow filled with succulent plants. Skillful gardeners trimmed their box trees into geometric shapes, and the most artistic among them made sculptures of elephants and hippopotamuses out of the solid masses of their plants. There was something of the secular crèche about the whole thing, although it lacked a messiah to federate it.

Regrouping certainly was the order of the day. We didn't know whether it was the lawn mowers or the authorities that had started it, but the go-ahead had been given to put an end to the suspicion of obscurantism and backwardness hanging over the region. Substitute order for chaos, light for shade, white snow for mud. The rural civilization passed the word around: We aren't peasants any longer. You've got the message, said the savior from the ministry that was united in its determination to raze the area: You are small farmers.

We were able to turn this to our advantage. The powerful bulldozers unearthed stones galore. One Sunday, this led to gleaning our best harvest yet among the unwanted debris of "*finis terrae*." Early that afternoon we had toured the Carnac Alignments. This was not the first time that our very own Le Nôtre had sought inspiration from the landscape gardeners of the Neolithic period. When his route passed the site, if he had a little time he would stop, walk a few steps among the menhirs, and then, sitting down on a fallen stone, fish out his pack of Gitanes and pensively smoke a cigarette, after automatically tapping it on his thumbnail to push down the tobacco. He claimed he felt in harmony with the tall steles gangrened by time and the elements, turning

up the collar of his jacket when the wind freshened, running
a hand through his hair when a slight drizzle sent him back
to his car. He would sit there for a moment, watching the
seabirds hover, the sparrows flutter above the heather, and,
between two puffs of smoke, his neck stretched up toward
the sky, he would try to solve the incomprehensible enigma
of this faceless statuary. As he had done some research, he
was aware that no one knew much about the question,
which put him on equal terms with the most eminent specialists of megalithic architecture. For an autodidact, whose
every reflection was thwarted by the authority of the
scholars, this was a godsend. In such cases he could let his
mind wander with impunity. Among the theories on the
meaning of the alignments, from the most serious to the
most fanciful, he gave no credit to the idea of landing strips
for Martian aircraft, though he was fascinated by the hy-
pothesis of a cosmic calendar capable of fixing the date of
the harvests and commemorating the birthday of the
prince, a sort of gigantic almanac that lacked only the
names of the saints carved on the stones and a few garden-
ing tips on the art and manner of cutting and arranging such
granite bouquets. Although a bit cumbersome and inconve-
nient to handle, this ephemeris for the birds — seeing that
they could only consult the sky — at least had the advantage of opening up vast horizons to reverie, and satisfied a
very real talent for mathematics, if we can judge by the ease
with which he solved the difficult problems we brought
home from school. This interpretation of Carnac presented
the world with a coded allegory. Everything had been said,
foreseen, enciphered: all you had to do was measure. As he
always carried a tape measure with him to check the diame-
ter of the glasses and flower pots, he had noted down the
distance between several menhirs that, five thousand years

before the master, were supposed to reproduce the ideal ratio set out in Pythagoras's theorem: three, four, five. But the results had turned out to be too random for anyone to be able to predict the day and time of the next eclipse with any accuracy. On one occasion he had even planned to watch the sun rise above the moor at the Kermario Alignment outside Carnac on the June solstice. According to the tales of the odd early risers, pseudo-druids, or neo-followers of Ra, the first ray scrupulously followed one pathway until it planted itself right in the middle of a cromlech, which, like the door of the Holy Sepulcher, represented the world and was rebaptized the Telluric-Axial Point of the Universe. But since the same ray was expected in several places at the same time, because it also had to cross the Merchants' Table in Locmariaquer, perforate the tumulus on the Island of Gavrinis, and also appear at the top of some other tall menhir, it was obvious that it couldn't satisfy everyone. On the previous evening the sky had been overcast, and when in the middle of the night in his little hotel room near Auray he had heard rain, he wisely switched off his alarm clock and preferred to go back to sleep.

Visitors were met on the site by troops of children who clustered around them and without any preliminaries started to intone a sort of lament, not one word of which was comprehensible. They churned it out in rapid monotones, as if they were reciting fables or the articles of the catechism, with the voice falling at the end of each phrase, which obliged the little officiants to keep taking noisy breaths before embarking on the next phrase. What was it all about? We found out much later: it was the legend of Saint Cornély, who, pursued by the Roman legions, was only saved by the intervention of the Lord, whose sacred breath had turned this army of assailants into stone statues. The government of the day hadn't thought of repatriating them, as is usual with the bodies of soldiers, and we were very glad of it because, apart from their removal being a tricky business, it would have meant the end of Carnac. But at the time, although we listened with all our ears, and did manage to catch a couple of identifiable syllables on the wing and put them together to reconstitute a word, it was extremely difficult to render unto Caesar his legions, and unto God his petrifying breath. As a result the mystery of the standing stones thickened and was coupled with a further question: What language were they expressing themselves in? in the Auray patois? in Gallo-Vannetois? in proto-Gallic? in low Latin? in pig Latin? in low Breton? in musical comedy Breton? It was Greek to us. Unless, possessed by a phenomenon inherent in that haunted place, moved by one of those secret turns of mind that can even manage to make tables speak, what came out of the mouths of the mediumistic little bards was the original language of the ancient builders, like a delayed action echo sent back by the stone walls. However that may be, these children were not slow on the uptake, because the moment their anthem was finished they held out their hands in the pure tradition of "don't forget the guide." Then the fathers would open their purses and halfheartedly search for the coin they judged adequate to reward the singing and the music. Because with regard to the part that interested us, the words, we were far from having had our fill. Then someone remarked that it was the same with opera, you never understood what they were saying, although considering the general ineptitude of the text this was just as well. All the emotion was transmitted through the music. Applied to our little choristers, whose monotonous notes didn't allow the slightest depth of

feeling to filter through, such a remark made you think that
the solid architects of the savage ages must have had hearts
of stone.

We were never to learn any more. After that, we all tried
to work it out for ourselves by strolling up and down the
pathways, the children providing the beginnings of a solution by climbing onto everything they found climbable. Our
very own Creator-Designer insisted on the size of the
stones, the difficulty of moving, sometimes over many kilometers, such considerable masses. All the more so in that
the same thing applied to menhirs as to icebergs — you also
had to consider the buried part that ensured the stability of
the block. If he insisted so much on what we couldn't see, it
was of course because invisible things open on infinity, but
it was also because we were finding it difficult to work up
much enthusiasm. Prepared by our great man, we were
expecting to see a field full of Eiffel Towers, and skyscrapers
of carved stone, instead of which no more than a handful of
them managed to rise to twelve feet. And even then, it was
better to be small yourself.

There is no improvisation in Carnac. It isn't like towns
that have gradually grown rich, like Venice or Amsterdam,
where merchants and bankers, as the years went by and as
the fancy took them, were constantly trying to outdo each
other with more beautiful, bigger, and flashier buildings
than those of their rivals. But here in Carnac, a single
project had been conceived and carried to term. And in a
very short time: if it had been spread over some decades the
initial plan, like that of a cathedral, would have been mod-
ified a hundred times. The recipe is simple: strong arms, an
efficient foreman, an inspired architect, and a tyrannical
prince. That's enough. The stones, erected within a couple
of steps of the coast as if to form a rampart against the

violence of the waves and the furious sea wind, are regularly spaced, orientated from east to west, and aligned in eleven or thirteen rows in decreasing order. If they were hollow, you could imagine fitting them one into the other like Russian dolls.

With time, many of them have disappeared: sold, reused, taking refuge in the wall of a fisherman's house or enclosing a pasture — the smallest ones at first, the easiest to move, the ones at the end of the row. If the order had been respected, the final stone in these alignments ought to have been the size of a grain of sand, a progressive dissolution into Mother Earth, or, starting from the east, a little grain of stone, a mineral seedbed, ending in the forest of the giants in the west. It was where this theoretical grain of sand would have been that we discovered, in the short grass near a tuft of sea pinks, the sort that grow along the Atlantic Coast, the corpse of a bird: its little body was emaciated, its neck bare as if death had removed its scarf; it had a bluish speck on its eye, a half-open beak, and its little vermicelli legs were folded like the frame of a dainty parasol. A few feathers still sticking to the fragile skeleton of its wing were flapping gently in the breeze.

Father knelt down by the tiny corpse, the better to observe it, no doubt, but in an attitude that was so reverent, so full of commiseration, that we imitated him and formed a circle around it, Mother being the only one to remain on her feet. We were on the threshold of a miracle of childish simplicity, convinced that Father was going to breathe life into the miniature breast, that its flesh would heal, its wings would beat again and then carry the rejuvenated bird up into the sky. As when the tombs of the blessed are opened, from these few grams of decomposed flesh there arose the sweet fragrance of the sea pinks. This perfumed message brought hope and consolation.

When he raised his head, Father's gaze fell upon the line of stones gently climbing toward the setting sun. Resting his arms on his knees, like a soccer player in the front row of a group photo, in his mind's eye he seemed to be following the flight of the bird above the alignments. The golden light soon forced him to lower his eyes. He shook his head pensively, and, as if he had been afraid of abandoning us, as a way of getting us to share his impressions, he said, "Even so, it does look very much like a cemetery."

Whereupon he stood up again, and kept our attention with a wink. He took the tape measure out of his pocket, measured the distance between the last two menhirs in the line, and at the same distance from the one at the end of the row made a mark on the ground with the toe of his shoe. He bent over again, and with his penknife, a stainless steel knife that he took everywhere and which had two blades plus a spike and a corkscrew, dug a hole as deep as a fist at the spot marked, cut a cardboard rectangle out of his cigarette pack, slid it under the bird's body, and deposited the whole in the little grave with all the caution of a porcelain salesman. Now that his cigarettes were loose in his pocket, he removed the silver paper they were wrapped in and used it as a luxurious shroud to cover the little victim.

After a rapid survey of the surroundings, he spotted a stone at the bottom of a clump of broom at the side of the field, carried it a few yards, and planted it vertically above the improvised tomb, thus completing the work of the long-gone gravediggers.

While we were silently attending the funeral ceremony, we didn't need to confer with one another to know that we were all thinking the same thing — the mound at the bottom of our garden under which the body of our last dog lay. A magnificent German shepherd whose love was exclusive, who used to lie on the mat inside the shop door, and whenever he was on his own put all the clients to flight: all he had to do was get to his feet, his head hunched up between his shoulders, his shoulder blades sticking out. If the person persisted, a low-frequency growl completed the message. There was, however, an Open Sesame. If he was called by his name he stopped his threats and lay down again heavily. Habitués cautiously pushed the door open a crack, called "Varus" in an uncertain voice, and he would even go up to some of them and beg to be caressed. There was great pride among those whom the big wolflike dog admitted into his inner circle. There was great relief when they buried their fingers in the beautiful animal's thick fur, patted his flanks, or massaged his throat, not without drawing on whatever reserves of courage they could find within themselves.

There were great difficulties for the shop, which already found it hard enough to get new customers, even though at the time the great majority of them were local residents — including the gypsies, also known as Bohemians, who had settled on some wasteland on the outskirts of the village. The women in their long dresses in definitely unfashionable colors yelled as they pushed the door open: "Tie that dog up!" and while they were cursing and swearing a few knick-knacks that happened to be handy would get tucked under their thick skirts — simply for the beauty of the gesture, because we would often find them in a ditch, where they'd been tossed with a magnificent contempt that we found insulting to our beautiful crockery.

With our Cerberus at the door, the household was well guarded. As Varus grew older, his love for all of us who belonged to him became more intense, but that only made him more unreasonable. Since our old Marie didn't live with us, she remained on the periphery of his affection. Her little house in the garden gave her the special status of a permanent guest. She didn't have to make herself known to the big dog, she could come and go freely without having to use his name as a password, but owing to her awkward ways with both animals and children, she didn't quite seem to be one of us. One afternoon in late summer while she was planning to take us for a picnic in the country, she intimated to the big dog that he was to stay at home, but he couldn't allow the children for whom he felt answerable to be thus removed from his care. So, as we were getting ready to leave, he jumped up at the old schoolmistress's arm.

The return of the responsible father was tragic. Our little aunt, her arm in a sling, tried hard to intervene, arguing that it wasn't serious, just a few stitches, and she'd hardly felt a thing. Father went upstairs, opened a drawer in the chest, grabbed his wartime gun — the one with which (a famous episode in our family mythology) he had forced his way through a German roadblock — and led the dog out to the bottom of the garden.

Later, he told anyone who could bear to listen, that his arm had faltered when he saw the animal's imploring gaze, with all the incomprehension in the world concentrated in the dark pupil staring at him — So this is my reward for all the love I've lavished on you — and then incomprehension turned into revolt, his gaze became ferocious, he bared his teeth, his growl rose in a crescendo, but just as the dog was about to spring Father's hand became steady again and he pressed the trigger. The explosion echoed around the tall brick walls. "Tres de mayo" in our garden. The gun, which

The next trip was fatal to the Dyna. This time we had been promised a surprise. The collector of ancient stones had shrouded in mystery the brass-headed stud stuck in the heart of Brittany. At that spot, there was nothing on the map, or at least on what we could read of it — the red main roads, the yellow secondary ones, the green-bordered ones of particular interest to tourists — to indicate anything special. It wasn't even a hamlet, it was just a place in the remote countryside near the narrow loop of a river, the Blavet no doubt, where the old granite substratum forces the streams into erratic detours. We stopped halfway for lunch at one of his favorite restaurants in which, after he had made a point of announcing our presence, we were served a meal that corresponded less to the day's menu than to his preferences. Thus, when the people at the next table coveted our chocolate mousse, they were told with some glee that it didn't exist. And, menu in hand: "Plum flan, apple tart, sherbet — where did you see mousse?" This kind of favoritism was a little disturbing, because it implied that during the week other women danced attendance upon him and that there were a lot of cooks along his way who prepared his favorite dishes, whereas it seemed to us that this role belonged to Mother alone. Everywhere in his wake we were welcomed as the emperor, his wife, and the little prince and princesses. He seemed pleased to introduce us, to allow us to benefit from his fame, convinced that it reflected back on us, which was quite true, as we realized after his death, although then it didn't do us any good, but at the time we would have preferred less partiality and more anonymity. Everything that conspired to make him an illustrious man — his strength of character, his sunny nature, his feeling for words — reminded us of the difficulty we experienced in growing up in his shadow. For other people, he was the man whose next visit they looked forward to, a promise of spring, a bird of passage. For us, he was the master of the house.

To reconstruct this weekday life of his that he led so far away from us, all we had were the names with which he peppered his stories: names of people, places, hotels that, in the absence of any reference points, took on mythical dimensions in our eyes. He reigned over a fabulous geography: Pont-Aven, Vannes, Quimper, Péaule, Roscoff, Rosporden, Landivisiau, Hennebont, Loudéac. The tiniest village took on an exotic charge when he spoke of it. On our trips with him, the illusion remained. As if by his mere presence he had the power of aggrandizing everything. And yet we were in a position to maintain that the towns we drove through were pervaded with a sense of boredom and sadness, that the hotels were modest, and that hotel cooking wasn't always as good as Mother's.

Wherever we stopped we were given an extra special welcome, which gave us the feeling of being considerable personalities, and we were told in confidence, as proof there was nothing to hide, a few fragments about his nomadic life. Our informant would come up to our table just as we were starting on the dessert and inquire, "Is everything all right?" — which was all the more self-assured in that he knew he had looked after us very well. He would tell us of an unusual man who on some evenings would stay behind to chat, pulling several tables together, inviting people on their own to join him, suggesting a game of cards, but who on other evenings would go up to his room early to bring his order forms up to date or simply to read, if he felt tired. We were confirmed in what we already knew, that he avoided political discussions. When people ventured to ask him his opinion, he would answer, "My politics is sport," which was less a profession of faith than an elegant, and perhaps evasive, way of cutting short the kind of debate in which passions get out of hand and vows of friendship are smashed to smithereens. He would invariably put an end to such differences of opinion by saying "There are better things to do," in which we recognized him as we knew him, because he had spent his whole life doing things — doing things, making things, achieving things. He made his first piece of furniture when he was twelve; he made a magic lantern to amuse his friends, tracing on grease-proof paper several of the adventures of the mischievous comic strip character Bicot, playing all the parts himself; he did a circus turn with Flip, a black and white ratter, the companion of his adolescence (famous photo taken during a youth club entertainment in which, with glasses on their noses and cigarettes in their mouths, they are both reading the same newspaper). He produced children (three of whom sur-vived); he covered kilometers (fifty thousand a year); he founded associations. At thirteen he was already the trea-surer of the Random Soccer Club, which he and some of his pals had started. The pals — as he captioned a later photo in which a group of beaming boys are posing in total chaos, some in shorts, others with their trousers hitched up to their knees, and all fighting to get hold of the ball. He stands behind them, dressed in a suit and tie, holding a cigarette between his fingertips with the elegance of James Bond holding his revolver. He is smiling, amused, quite simply happy to have worked toward the success of this instant. His round-rimmed spectacles, the kind worn by severe intellectuals, seem to keep him aloof from the general euphoria, as if he were afraid they might get broken in the merrymaking. According to the date written on the back of the photo he was sixteen, and already just over six feet tall, which makes him tower over the group.

Did the elegant young man with the cigarette suffer from not feeling quite at home in this remote part of the country-side where he was born, did he suffer from forcing the friendship of his companions in an effort to convince him-self of the opposite, and from trying to deploy his enormous talents within the very little that life was prepared to grant him? Did the thought sometimes cross his mind that if he had been better served by events and by the accident of birth he would have deserved a better fate? Looking at him in this photo, you find yourself dreaming of a glorious future for this handsome, enterprising young man, now that Munich has dispersed the clouds, that the specter of war is retreating, and that peace has been guaranteed for a thousand years. But for the moment it seems that the most important thing for him is not to be alone. There are quite a few who remember painfully that he can't bear to be called an only son — perhaps the only occasion on which he used his fists. He thought of his stillborn or miscarried brothers and sisters as if such an insult was a reproach to him for having survived this child carnage. Did he feel so much an orphan that throughout his life he tried so hard to become part of a family? Later, he set up a theater company, whose crowning achievement was the memorable performance of *The Three Musketeers* in occupied Random. After that he organized the reunion of the "forty-year-olds," and for this, so that all his age group could take part, so that no one should be excluded, not even the least presentable, the inveterate alcoholics or the near-tramps, he put his hand in his own pocket and paid for the traveling expenses and meals of the most indigent among them. André and his wife, two magnificent wrecks who had met and found the consolation of love while being dried out at the Pont-de-Pitié Hospital, and who are standing next to him hand in hand in the souvenir photo of the group of these new forty-year-olds, looking older than their age, of course — every year of hardship counts double — but radiant, André seigneurial, looking like a responsible man, in a check suit and with his hair tousled, Odette, with a coquettish look in her eye but with the gaps in her teeth revealed by her big smile, in a jersey dress whose shabbiness is betrayed by the bulges beneath her knees, wearing what is probably her only piece of jewelry, her First Communion crucifix no doubt, because for such an event even the poorest don't consider the expense, both of them proud of the respect shown them by Joseph the Great, under his protection recognized, adopted — part of the family, in short. He, Joseph, a whole head taller, is wearing an open-neck shirt, which makes him look relaxed, and his smile is just the same as it was twenty-four years earlier although less reserved, as if he had decided that his place was here, among these people — and anyway, he's considering the proposition of the director of the little Random hospital who is just coming up to retirement age and has suggested him as his successor — smiling one of his last smiles that hasn't been distorted by suffering.

After the chocolate mousse, we got back into the Dyna and drove off in the direction of Malestroit, where we wandered about among the old Gothic and Renaissance half-timbered houses with the grotesque carvings on their facades, one with a strange pelican, like in the comic strip we delighted in, and then stopped at the convent where we admired the little Lord Jesus as he appeared to a novice in ecstasy: pink, wearing an exiguous diaper, and with Alexandrian curls over his forehead. Lying on his golden straw, he is opening his arms like His Holiness the Pope and raising his head, which demands a strenuous effort of the back of the neck and the abdominal muscles of which only babies with a great destiny in store seem capable. At the entrance, we bought a postcard, which when we got home Father presented to his pious aunt, our universal Aunt Marie, who lost no time in inserting the beloved image into one of her innumerable prayer books. Perhaps he was forestalling the reproaches that she would not fail to heap upon him when she discovered what we were bringing back, what in fact had been the reason for our journey: our loot.

We had started off again through the labyrinth of the Breton countryside. The powerful bulldozers on this Sunday "day of rest" were getting their breath back near a hedge they had flattened, their shovels resting on the ground, their red mass standing out like great bleeding gashes against the dark green of the landscape. The sky was overcast; it was drizzling. Through the regular to-ing and fro-ing of the windshield wipers, the driver pointed to a chapel spire rising up from the yellow palette of a field of colza. The roar of the engine rendered explanations impossible, but by the way he emphasized his gesture we realized that we were reaching our goal.

The granite spire surmounted a massive tower separated from the chapel, which lay in the hollow of an amphitheater of greenery, so that as you approached you could imagine it was half buried, a victim of its own mass or of a landslide, and this foreshortening of its walls made it look even more like a reliquary, a box of precious bones. The little path, which had been annexed by the hens from a neighboring farm, was on a level with its stained-glass windows. If you had taken it at a run, with a slightly perilous leap you could have reached its cornice and the smiling angel, wearing a saucy little hat of green moss, who seemed to have taken refuge on the roof in anticipation of the day when the church would be engulfed for good. We walked down the stone steps leading to the chapel. Its entrance was guarded by a fountain whose overflow ran into three ponds in the shape of an ace of clubs. In a rusty tin can, there was a bunch of nearly dead wildflowers. Instead of entering through the porch, we walked around the building down the little path squeezed between the wall and the embankment along the road until we came to the apse, whose base was invaded by clumps of hydrangea. Our guide asked us to pull the big blue flowers away from the wall. Mother warned us, you'll get wet, and when we hesitated, he decided to plunge into the dripping flowers — Joseph, you'll get dirty—then got a grip on something heavy, leaned backward with all his weight, trying to get a solid foothold on the slippery grass — Joseph, you're mad — and began to lug a huge stone out of the bush, rolling it over and over. In actual fact it was a truncated pyramidal block, and now that we could get a better look at it, we saw that it was a carved capital whose patterns and figures had been eroded by time and didn't come from the chapel — which was itself perfectly preserved and as far as we could see all in one piece — but perhaps came from an earlier building. It could have been judged too barbaric to be reused, not refined enough for the elegance of the Renaissance, and abandoned near the site where our gold miner had dug it out and promptly hidden it, immediately imagining how he could turn it to account, this time not seeing it as something to add to the chaos of the stones casually dumped between the plants in our rockery, but as a part of history, thus obliging the long march of civilization to make a little detour through our garden. This prestigious gesture would call attention to the fact that we all, whether clog makers or stonecutters, have a right to our share of recognition.

At the bottom of the garden, between our aunt's little house and the garage, in the middle of an empty space surrounded by high walls, there are four reinforced-concrete poles, crowned with iron spikes and arranged in a square, which seem to mark the perimeter of an atrium or a cloister. They were originally intended to support the roof of a vast warehouse, the old one being thought much too small. This ambitious plan for future expansion had been interrupted by the war (the second one), by the death of the planner (Pierre, Joseph's father and Marie's brother), and by the recent and more rigorous system of taxation (before 1939, Pierre only had to pay for a business license and refused to contribute to the tax levied to finance the war effort, considering that he had already given quite enough to war — four years in the trenches, for which his reward was an ex-serviceman's pension that just about covered his yearly expenditure on tobacco). And the most telling reason for the abandonment of the project was that the more times changed, the more untenable became the situation of wholesalers in small rural communities. Now that the improvement of the roads had reduced the necessity for middlemen between manufacturers and retailers, this was no time to increase your stock and risk having it left on your hands.

Along with the concrete poles, there remains another vestige of the marvelous grandpaternal project: a portico of hollow bricks on a concrete framework that was to have covered its entrance. At the sight of this strange construction, the eye hesitates. Is it a ruined building, a small abandoned factory, dating from between the wars? Or an unfinished piece of architecture? And the roof? Blown off or never put on? The high walls force you to raise your eyes. The absence of any roofing reveals a wide rectangle of sky, with the tapering top of a cypress tree piercing it like a paintbrush. It contains very little blue that might make you hope for a vertical glimpse of the infinite beyond, and what patches of blue there are seem like mere puddles among the massive clouds that come billowing in from the Atlantic, or which unravel, not having been properly carded, or which, frothy little clue, herald the rainy days to come. A parsimonious, pale, fresco-like blue. A miserly blue, compared to the dazzling splendor of the grays, which range from pearl to ash, from chinchilla to soot, an ever-changing wash superimposed on the mists. If watching the passage of the clouds makes you feel dizzy, look down, open an oyster, decorticate a mussel: all the variegated hues of the Atlantic are registered in the mother-of-pearl of these shellfish. In the summer, this meadow-in-the-sky at the bottom of our garden is invaded by colonies of swifts and swallows that establish their second residence in the roof of the church and spend their holidays describing playful arabesques in the sky, a supple corporate body undulating like paramecia and filling the handful of fine days with their strident little cries. When you look down again, you catch another glimpse of the metal spikes sticking out of the concrete poles. This is a sign. A clear sign that the work really is unfinished.

Joseph's idea was Herculean. As he explained to us, he was going to saw off the spikes, disguise the poles as columns, and make the top of one of them the resting place for the capital that had been waiting in the Breton soil for some five or six centuries, hoping to regain its height. In the center, between the four columns, he was going to dig a shallow basin and line it with mosaic or bits of broken crockery. Just imagine, Hadrian's villa in our garden! The great audacious architect was going to mix centuries and styles and finish off the unfinished building by turning it into a ruin. When our aunt's pious statuettes had been embedded in the wall to perfect the picture, no one would have any idea of what was what, or which god they were supposed to worship. Over Random, on the map of Brittany, we would stick a diamond-headed pin.

The dreams of "Joseph, you're mad" were on the grand scale, and he had now started to roll the heavy stone over toward the steps, first one side then the next, repeating the operation twenty or thirty times, and when one of its beveled sides made the capital deviate from a straight line, he had to shove it back again. Then he started heaving it up the narrow steps one at a time, but it was so precariously balanced — Joseph, be careful — that it looked as if it was going to topple down again and take him with it. Next he reversed the car until it was as close as possible, opened the trunk, removed a blanket and a can of oil, leaned over the stone, which was resting on its edge, slightly tilted, put his arms around it — Joseph, you'll get dirty — and, like a weight-lifter, took a deep breath before hoisting it off the ground, his jaws clenched, his face showing the extent of the effort, for a moment carrying his burden like a pregnant woman. As he carefully put it down when his trembling arms, if they had had their own way, would already have dropped it, the car suddenly slumped onto its back axle, and with his hands still on the stone he stood there for quite a time, trying to get his breath back, his eyelids lowered.

Then he straightened up and put a hand on his back — Joseph, you've hurt yourself — and we realized we must say nothing that would elicit a curt reaction from him but simply look at him in silence, the way you wait for a moment suspended in time to give a new sign of life.

Quite a few people were hovering around, giving the tires surreptitious little kicks, caressing the wings, glancing at the speedometer — it went up to 130 kilometers per hour, but all, except perhaps the owner, agreed that speedometers exaggerate — trying to pluck the remains of the blue film off the chromes, though when they pull at it in the hope of removing a long strip, instead of peeling off the film keeps shrinking until it forms a pointed tongue, which soon breaks. Nevertheless, this protective layer is proof positive that the car is new and not secondhand — which often seems a bit like a warmed-up dish or handed-down clothes — and has come straight from the factory still half enveloped in its translucent blue gift wrap. After the debacle of the Dyna coming home at a snail's pace along the Breton roads, making a deafening racket, the metallic-green Peugeot 403 parked outside the shop and coveted by all the bystanders is a delightful present. It's quite something to see the joy of the salesman when he gets behind the wheel and starts up the engine in front of his friends: they all bend their ears over the hood and, remembering the Dyna, pretend they can't hear a thing. What? That vague murmur is enough to power a car? It's also quite something to see his smile reflected in the windshield, and the way he gently presses the accelerator a couple of times to show his satisfaction.

The pack of Gitanes has naturally already found its place on the dashboard in front of the steering wheel. He takes one out and, instead of using his own lighter, proudly presses the cigarette lighter, which he then holds out the open door to the dumbfounded smokers. "Just a moment, that's not all." He also gives them a demonstration of the reclining back of his seat. "It's got everything but a shower," someone remarks. When he gets out of the car he walks around it again with the group, the cigarette in the corner of his mouth, and stops in front of the brand-new license plate: 917 GG 44. "GG for *grande gueule*," he says. Is that what he's afraid the others think of him? Why beat his breast in public? The shadow is soon dispersed, and everyone laughs at his joke.

In the peaceful War of the Roses being carried on at the beginning of the sixties between the supporters of Peugeot and Renault — although when you consider the victims of road accidents it was a bloody war — from now on we are on Peugeot's side. To the Renault fans who boast of the speed, responsiveness, and more athletic lines of the range of cars with the diamond logo, we oppose our own arguments: solidity, road-holding, reliability of the engine, and body-work that doesn't crumple up like an accordion. But to be on the safe side, Father screwed on to the dashboard a heavy bronze medal of the good Saint Christopher, which he had made sure of removing from the Dyna before she went to the junkyard. Which, for this man, was a little surprising. Heaven is primarily the business of women. Was it to please his devout Aunt Marie? Whatever, the Peugeot 403 is a decent, unpretentious car that can be relied on. Like him. They would understand each other. This new comfort will mean the end of his problems and the relief of his back pains, which have recently been getting more acute. Too many suitcases to be handled, and those useless stones he piles up in his garden. He won't recognize, not him, that he may perhaps have overtaxed his strength. And who would dare to suggest as much? You might as well reproach him for working himself to death for his family. For what he really wants is that his family should live beyond his means; that's his duty as a father and husband, regardless of the expense.

But with such an acquisition, everything would be all right now. And indeed, the gallant 403 did take him up to the mythical hundred-thousand-kilometer line he was so anxiously waiting for it to cross. When the clock had reset itself at zero, when its five virgin numerals were aligned, it would immediately wipe out ninety-nine thousand nine hundred and ninety-nine kilometers of Breton roads (there were no other journeys during this period), two years of hotels, of clients, of unpacking, of sales talk — a Faustian cure for the price of the reliability of an engine and a car's bodywork. Just a few more yards and nothing would have taken place, neither the separation, nor the solitary evenings, nor the hope of better days; just one more turn of the wheel and the world would be no more than a perpetual recommencement.

There. Perfect virginity of the clock. He pulls over to the side of the road, which overlooks a little valley where a bulldozer is desperately trying to transform a mosaic of tiny little fields into a plain in the Beauce. For some time now he has been telling us of his sadness and sense of helplessness at the sight of the countryside being tortured under his very eyes. His anger, sometimes. Where, in this future desert, will he find new landmarks? Every tree was a beacon in his personal geography, and at this or that intersection, with its roadside shrine — with which Brittany abounds, and in front of which many women cross themselves — his car would head in the right direction as if of its own accord, a field of gorse would herald the spring more surely than the color of the sky, and a certain church steeple that used to rise above the hedges now seems undressed and can be seen from so far away that you no longer bother to make a detour to satisfy your curiosity. This furious clean sweep of the great work of the men of the land — do you attack the gardens of Vaux-le-Vicomte? — was the same as if someone had cruelly torn the pins with the colored heads off his wall map. Just because the clock has reset itself at zero, does that mean the whole landscape also has to be wiped out?

He switches off his engine. The ensuing silence is immediately invaded by the parasitical hum of the mechanical digger in the distance. Now he's ready for action, and he has already premeditated the consequence of this action. He told us about it later, which showed the fine independence of his mind, because his tale was so typical of the female of the species that no one who was supposed to be a big shot or a tough guy would dare confess it. It was the kind of bargain that people sometimes strike to guarantee their future: If things work out the way I hope they will, I promise to do this or that — stay sober, smile at the neighbor's cat, swallow endless insults, go on a pilgrimage to Jerusalem on my knees — the offers vary according to the importance of the bargain. The moment has now come when he must keep his word. But it is so difficult to look at oneself objectively, as if one were a character in a play, and to forget one's dignity. One observes oneself, and is paralyzed. He temporizes by lighting a cigarette.

The afternoon is coming to a gentle close, the hazy sky is diffusing a soothing light over the Breton countryside, like a healing balm over the devastated fields. The tall mounds of earth pushed back against the sides of the valley are already covered in foxgloves and bramble bushes and have been swarming with activity ever since the exiles from the hedges chose to make their nests there. A few cows amble up the meadow and stick their heads over the hedge to keep up with the latest news. He lowers the window, the smoke escapes. It has become so hot inside the car with the heat turned up to the maximum that the softness of the air makes him shiver. Gradually, the scents of grass and hawthorn come in and mingle with the foul smell of stale smoke permeating the car. He still hesitates. Just as he flicks his cigarette butt out the window to the other side of the road there is a sign, a miracle, whatever might have been said about it by those who saw it only as the end of a day's work: the mechanical digger falls silent and suddenly surrenders the surroundings to their natural sounds — the birds singing as they take flight, the branch and leaves slightly trembling, the hedge quivering at the touch of the massive hindquarters of the cows; their plodding feet; the muffled echoes from a farm; and in the peace of the approaching evening, he thanks the heavens for having accompanied him throughout these hundred thousand kilometers without any other problems than the normal running repairs, without the slightest accident either to himself or to his family, and he gives thanks for being alive. He recites an Our Father and three Hail Marys.

This would have been as simple as ABC for our little aunt, but coming from him no one would ever have believed it. Not that he set himself up as a free thinker, but his remarks on religion were tinged with a discreet anticlericalism that upset our old Marie, who divided her time between the convent school where she taught and the church. She was not only a regular attendant at its services, she was also in some way responsible for its maintenance, and in particular for the collection boxes, and this, for we who had the privilege of accompanying her when she emptied them on

Sunday evenings, seemed to be very like larceny with a key — the feverish discovery when the little wooden door was opened of the pile of coins inserted through the slot (small change and buttons), which we clawed out and put into a canvas bag, taking care not to let any of them fall on the floor, then checking in the corners in case we'd left some behind, and thus box by box adding to our booty, the bag becoming heavier and heavier in our hands, our lawful thieves' footsteps resounding in the scary half-light of the church. But our aunt avoided arguments with her nephew. In the first place because she loved him, and furthermore because there can be no discussion about the Church, its dogmas, and its servants. She preferred to put a stop to any such talk by shrugging and, turning on her heel, trotting off, her head lowered, muttering to herself. It was useless for him to remind her that the nuns whom she championed so fiercely had made things so difficult for her during her career as a schoolmistress that, at her brother's suggestion, she had even agreed to leave her room at the school and come and live in the little house he'd had built for her in the garden. She must have felt she was deserting them. She knew all this, of course she did. There was no need to rub salt in the wound. She still sometimes came back from the school on the verge of tears because the Mother Superior had made an unkind remark. But that was her business. It was not for her to sit in judgment on those women who had dedicated their lives to the service of Christ when she herself, after all, however pious she might be, had never taken the veil. Perhaps this was her way of paying for her evasion. On the other hand, she had no hesitation in pointing out to her recalcitrant nephew that Easter was approaching and that the confessionals were waiting for him because it was spring-cleaning time. Even though he only made up his mind at the last moment, he did yield to this annual check-up, and, it seems, with no apparent metaphysical torment. This never failed to cause us some alarm as to the salvation of his soul. It was his religious observance, which in our eyes was extremely vacillating, that had led us to classify him, if not among the unbelievers, at least among the very amateurish category of people who are believers out of habit or obligation. We were convinced that not going to Mass on Sundays, just like chewing the Host or blaspheming (even though we had no idea how to do that), was to put yourself in a state of mortal sin. And he was playing with fire, arriving well after the Introit, when the sermon was already well under way (it was always boring, according to him, and yet Father Bideau, the curé, from the height of his pulpit presented us with a terrifying vision of hell, and, his eyes bulging, leaning so far forward that his teeth sometimes came into collision with the microphone, hammered out in a voice that seemed to come from beyond the grave the words "Oh, the demon, oh, the wicked demon," as if he could espy the demon in the modest décolletés of the women sitting below him but after such an admonition we lost all inclination to behave like little demons). Father, meanwhile, would be standing near the door, by the font, and sometimes, toward the end, leaning against a pillar (at this period the church was never empty and there was no question of walking up the aisle in search of an empty chair, especially if you happened to be wearing squeaky patent leather shoes — unless of course you wanted people to notice them), and he would take advantage of the confusion at the time of the communion and the comings and goings in the side aisles to slip out before everyone else, when the sound of the door creaking was drowned by the organ and five hundred people bawling at the top of their voices: "I am a Christian, therein lies my glory, my hope and my support." All of which reduced his attendance at divine service to not much more than a quarter of an hour. We were afraid that that wasn't enough.

To tell the truth, he wasn't the only one who acted in this way. It was the hallmark of the men in general, many of whom, not wanting to remain standing even though they'd arrived late, found it convenient to borrow chairs from the cafés in the square and carry them into the back of the church. So a curious ballet took place in the little town every Sunday. Some of the men, prematurely tipsy, found it difficult to get through the revolving door at the side entrance without bumping their chairs against its wooden panels, thus disturbing the great solemn silence of the offertory and incurring the wrath of Bideau, who took his eyes off the ciborium in order to identify the culprit and rebuke him at the next opportunity. But these reprimands were also part of the ritual. They were proof that one was a member of the men's clan. People even cast doubt on the virility of those who didn't miss a moment of the Mass. They installed themselves in the front row from the first sound of the bell, an open missal in their hands and hymns in their mouths — but this presumption of impotence was certainly unjust to one of them, who had the face of a Mormon preacher, only one wife, and ten children.

The caste of the devout often included former seminarians who had been led astray by the call of sex. We remembered having seen some of them who had once worn the cassock but who had abandoned it just before they were to have been ordained. Having been recruited into the ecclesiastical network when very young (for the poorest among

them this guaranteed an education with all its ensuing pres-
tige), they had discovered late in the day that they hadn't
been told everything. Nevertheless they retained their original faith and talked their children into resuming the path
they themselves had forsaken, but the children didn't wait
as long as their fathers before permanently choosing ag-
nosticism.

Corpus Christi was the occasion for Joseph the Great to
demonstrate his talents as an organizer and inventor. The
procession of the Blessed Sacrament followed a path strewn
with flower petals that, because of late flowering, were most
often replaced by wood shavings of different colors, strung
out in a long ribbon of gaudy geometrical patterns through
the streets of the parish, and upon which Bideau, leading
with the monstrance, was the first to tread. Each district
was responsible for the decoration of its own sector. The
upper town district had the advantage of possessing within
its ranks, in the person of the charcutier, an authentic artist
capable of creating a Victory of Samothrace in lard or a
crèche in goose pâté. In purely aesthetic terms, it was out of
the question for us to try to compete, with our reproduction
of a Christ in Majesty in his flowered halo. So we confined
ourselves to a rudimentary mosaic, with diamond shapes
and ornamental borders, embellished at a right angle with a
rosette, the sort schoolboys draw with their compasses
when they're bored.

Early that Sunday morning the volunteers got together
in the garage, its doors wide open to welcome onlookers,
part-time helpers who would muck in for ten minutes,
advisers (that's not the way to do it, you should do it like
this), the people who told true stories of run-over cats — or
more likely hens, which, being more stupid and less swift,
paid a heavy price to passing cars — those who were dying

of thirst (refreshment breaks had been planned for the fresco painters), the busybodies, and, as the morning wore on, the women and children.

The first phase consisted of diluting the dyes in big bowls and then filling the bowls with the wood shavings brought in cardboard boxes and wheelbarrows from the nearby carpenter's shop and stockpiled throughout the year in anticipation of the procession. People took turns to stir the mixture with a stick whose submerged tip became coated, according to the different bowls, in green, yellow, blue, or orange, acquiring a special status by this distinguishing mark, a sort of field marshal's baton that, instead of being burned or thrown away, was later recycled to act as a stake for a rosebush. You had to take care not to splash yourself when you were stirring this thick soup, because the dye was indelible and got ingrained under your fingernails. Those of us who thought it too womanish to wear gloves when we spread out the shavings still had a thin stripe of color in the lines of our hands for a long time afterward, which some seemed to be in no hurry to get rid of; holding out their open palms, it was a way of saying "I was there!" before starting to tell the tale of that joyous morning.

For the stenciled fresco, we used stretchers that looked something like sections of a railway track. The ties between the two wooden rails made rectangles that we merely had to fill with colored shavings. This done, four men delicately picked up the frame, taking care not to joggle the fragile mosaic, and joined it to the previous sections, repeating the operation until it reached our border with the neighboring district.

Cars that day were requested to make a detour, so as not to break the long multicolored ribbon, but this request didn't go unchallenged. The artists kneeling on the pave-

ment, bending over their design, conspicuously occupied
the middle of the road. Confident of their legitimacy, they
were certainly not prepared to be dislodged by repeated
horn blowing. To be on the safe side — and because Joseph
wanted to give him a part to play — André, already slightly
tipsy, was asked to direct the traffic, which, fortified by the
approval of the group and sure of his authority, he did,
putting two fingers in his mouth to whistle at offenders, and
even going so far as to dye his handkerchief red in one of the
tubs and wave it in front of the motorists' windshields to
indicate a no-go area.

The road running past the garage was regularly used by
a herd of cows that grazed in the luxuriant meadows in the
lower part of the town. You didn't have to be a partic-
ularly skilled tracker to see which way they'd gone. Ideally,
the best thing was to sweep the road before the procession
was due, but time was short that day, there weren't enough
shavings, so Joseph hurriedly made an improvised
stretcher out of two rafters held together by four cross-
pieces, in the meantime sending an army of volunteers to
trim the box and laurel trees in the garden. We'd barely
finished scattering their little round and spear-shaped
leaves alternately when the cortege came into view round-
ing the corner. We all lined up at the side of the road, our
arms crossed or our hands held one over the other like a
fig leaf, joining in each hymn or prayer as it went by,
adopting the appropriate air, contrite expression, and inspired gaze, when a perfidious spectator nudged his neighbor. When he had had time to react, he quickly passed on
the good news, which spread up the ranks like wildfire,
and our gravity fought a losing battle with the irrepressible
desire to laugh that was visible on everyone's face, some
biting their lips, others suddenly turning their backs, still

others choosing to break ranks in order to give free rein to their unseemly mirth, while Bideau, deep in meditation, holding the monstrance up in front of his face, moving at an inordinately slow pace over the carpet of green leaves, ceremoniously walked in cow dung.

Was it because he had premonitions, that for our last outing he insisted on taking us to visit Paris? It had been several years since we had gone on vacation, which, in spite of the statistics, didn't worry us all that much. We were quite happy to spend the summer within the high walls of the garden. It was going away, on the contrary, that bothered us. Not so much because we were leaving our familiar landmarks behind; it was more that we were suddenly exposed to other people's eyes — and they were all we were aware of. In restaurants they drew attention to the fact that you weren't holding your fork properly; in hotels, that you made too much noise walking down the corridors looking for your room; in a cable car, that your presence was likely to overload it, which made you feel like jumping out into the void; at the Cirque de Gavarnie, that you were walking up it while richer or bolder people rode up on muleback; at the Château de X, that you were quite wrong to think that du Guesclin's bed was very short and therefore deduce that he too must have been short; and, at La Bourboule, that you were equally wrong to make a face when you drank the arsenical spa waters. Naturally, it was the same watchful eyes that had always stopped us from going to the beach: our skin was too pale. Paris was even more intimidating. The decision to visit the capital had, it seems, been made hastily, almost on the spur of the moment, in the same way as he had one day come home at about ten in the evening, suddenly taken a notion to knock down a partition, and immediately started to demolish it with a hammer. The choice of Paris seemed all the more surprising in that our conversations didn't revolve like moths around the City of Light. This change of direction, after the severity of the Breton landscapes he had accustomed us to, was as if he were putting the life of the stones behind him and hoping to be flooded with light. Like an irradiant remission before the dark night.

He had spent his last few holidays repairing and making improvements to the house, lining and insulating the ceilings, repapering the bedrooms, arranging and enlarging the shop, giving it access to the basement so it had two levels, like in the town. That summer, according to his plans, which ranged from the necessary to the superfluous, he should have been starting on the garden. He had finally gotten together all the materials for his great project. Buried under the tall grass, the stones brought from Brittany had been awaiting their final destination for many months. The capital was covered in green moss. All the broken crockery had ended up in a crate, and we were beginning to doubt if it would ever pave the basin of a fountain. But, whether because the doctors had advised against it or because he had lost interest and didn't have the strength, he seemed to have decided to let his Babylonian reverie lie dormant.

The 403 was coming to the end of the road. After it had religiously crossed the hundred-thousand-kilometer line it had carried on for a few more months, but its exceptional longevity was actually an indication of its imminent demise. It was feeling the weight of the kilometers more and more. It was as greedy for oil as an old lady is for sweets. One after the other its parts succumbed, and Joseph would replace them on Sundays. We suspected that Paris would be the 403's swan song. In order to spare it, rather than driving the five hundred kilometers in one go, on the first evening we broke our journey between Chartres and Versailles. The next day, at a jog trot, we entered the capital.

Travelers are very often stationary travelers. They settle wherever planes and boats set them down. That was how the Breton immigrants came to inhabit the surroundings of the Gare Montparnasse. Our guide, who never did anything like anyone else, took us, on the contrary, to the Porte Dorée district, to a hotel whose shutters, lit by the streetlights, traced two luminous ladders on the bedroom ceiling. The incessant rumble of the cars going by until late at night was a bit like the familiar sound of the ocean. And, so that we shouldn't feel too disorientated, it was raining in Paris. Which wasn't at all to the liking of the animals in the nearby Vincennes Zoo, where we began our visit to the capital. Which wasn't to our liking, either, because as a result the animals had deserted the artificial rocks that provided them with their decor of an African operetta. We found some compensation in the polar bears and seals, who welcomed this August rain and dived into their dubious-looking pools as gracefully as mermaids. We walked slowly along the paths, deciphering the labels on the cages, testing our knowledge, pleased to confirm that the great lanky thing with the long speckled neck really was a giraffe. Although we were walking so slowly, Father kept stopping, letting us get a few paces ahead of him. Turning around, we could see pain written on his face. We saw him tip a few aspirins into his hand and swallow them without water, with a sudden backward toss of his head. Even the antics of the baby monkeys, which with three somersaults landed perched on their placid mothers' heads, couldn't make him smile. The only thing that got an amused grin from him was when a keeper, wearing an outsize cap, asked a group massed in front of a cage to move on, and after a silence added, "Make way for the stars!" Then, delighted with the impression he'd made, with a theatrical gesture he cracked an imaginary ringmaster's whip.

After this introduction to wildlife we were ready to confront the big city. Of the obligatory sights, we saw neither the Eiffel Tower — except for its silhouette, which looked like an overgrown derrick over the rooftops — nor the waxworks museum, nor the Sacré-Coeur, not even making a detour by way of the Moulin Rouge, the Cour Carrée of the Louvre, nor the Luxembourg Gardens. It was as if his schedule followed his thoughts: Notre-Dame, the Palace of Discovery, the Invalides, and, outside the city walls, a visit to the Château de Fontainebleau that, later, we found difficult not to interpret as a farewell ceremony.

Braving the Paris traffic with the 403 in its present state wouldn't have been reasonable. So, sticking closely to our great man, we plunged down into the métro. Once past the intimidating mob in front of the ticket windows, while we were deciding on our route we were pleasantly surprised to find ourselves on familiar ground: the electrified métro map — on which bulbs of different colors, each line having its own, light up at the touch of a button and indicate the ideal itinerary between two stations — was the counterpart, in a more sophisticated version, of his map of Brittany. Thanks to that we felt a bit less provincial, each of us unwittingly familiar with the capital, as if we were already in complete command of the very best method of traveling in Paris. We recognized this as his way of marking out our course, of preparing us by a series of signs for other worlds, like the shop on two levels, incongruous in a small community — the incessant warfare he carried on against routine and the inability of most people to challenge the existing order of things. He had no hesitation, for instance, in getting rid of two antique but not very practical armoires on the first floor landing and replacing them with a monumental storage unit he had himself designed. It was of doubtful elegance, but it met all our needs, from clothes closet to linen chest, and it possessed a system of interior lighting operated by opening and closing its doors.

But the similarity between the two maps was enough to set him dreaming; at the same time it acknowledged his creativity and cheated him of his invention. Tapping the keys corresponding to the stations, trying out the different combinations, he even let several people go before him so as not to be disturbed in his privileged dialogue with the machine. You didn't have to be much of a wizard to guess that he was studying the possibility of electrifying his map of Brittany in the same way: instead of map pins with different-colored heads and cotton thread replicating Ariadne's clue, a string of little Christmas tree lights would indicate his schedule for the coming week. For the modern man that he was, this was logical progress. But he made a funny little face, a contraction of his lips, which we took to mean that he had already given up on the idea. It wasn't in his line, that complicated network of connections and electric wires — or it was too involved, or he was suddenly overcome by lassitude. And after all, what was the point? Hadn't he already considered retiring, abandoning his long odyssey and accepting his friend's offer to succeed him as director of the Random hospital-cum-old-people's-home. There would be plenty of illuminated signs and flashing lights on the switchboard and in the staff room. There would be no shortage of opportunities to use his talents as an inventor. As for his future route, he would only have to walk three hundred yards. No need to put up an ordnance survey map in his office for that.

From the Porte Dorée to the Invalides was simple, too. No changes. Direct line. Presumably, the site of the monument had been judiciously chosen. We found a *Life of Napoleon* in the library, its jacket illustrated by Baron Gros's picture of a disheveled Bonaparte crossing the Bridge of Arcola and casting an anxious eye behind him, worried his men might not be following. Which indeed would have put a premature end to his career. But they did follow him. They followed him so well that he was now reposing, a cuckoo in the luxurious nest of Louis XIV, under Hardouin-Mansart's gigantic gilded dome, in his red porphyry mausoleum, delivered up to the curiosity of the crowd congregated at the railing of the circular gallery to admire the imperial ashes down below, in the center of the open crypt — even if in actual fact no one, not even the English, ever thought of cremating his body: it must have been the trauma of Joan of Arc. But "the ashes" sounds better than "the remains," which makes you think of the leftovers that no one ever knows what to do with. Although it's true that no one really knew what to do with the guest of Saint Helena. And yet, apart from this piece of workmanship, Napoleon didn't seem to occupy a very special place in our family pantheon, unless he held one for Cousin Rémi, whose birthday fell on the same day as the coronation and the battle of Austerlitz, a fact he never failed to remind us of every year, perhaps as a veiled response to his cousin Joseph who was born on 2 /22 /22 and who saw this remarkable sequence as a sort of mark of destiny, a magic formula, which it certainly wasn't when you consider his short lease on life.

But remembrances of Napoleon would probably not have been enough to get us to the Invalides had there not been a more deep-seated reason for our visit. After Father had leaned over the imperial tomb for a few moments, and without even lingering over the pompous bas-reliefs in the crypt representing the new Christ-king surrounded by his generals as if they were apostles, he began to examine the hundreds of flags displayed in the church, in search of the one of the seventh regiment of dragoons, to which his father had belonged. After years of war, a dragoon in a trench looks no different from any other poilu — French recruit — overwhelmed by cold and suffering. The photo of Pierre taken at the front, his blue uniform covered in mud, but smiling in spite of everything so as not to worry his family, hasn't a great deal in common with the one taken when he was in training a few years before the war, which shows him wearing a helmet with a long plume, his sword by his side, thrusting out his chest in his beautiful frogged uniform with the two embroidered 7's on the collar. But when you see the name of the person this photo was dedicated to, you realize that the main purpose of his noble bearing was to captivate his betrothed and future spouse. The quartermaster sergeant who, in another photo taken at the same period, is seen posing in high spirits with his comrades in arms in front of the horseshoe staircase leading up to the Château de Fontainebleau, the town where his regiment was based, probably never for a moment imagined that the mischief his squadron got into would one day result in a theater of horror. From his four years at the front, he was to bring back a profound distaste for all things military that he communicated to his son, who, drafted into the regular army after his two years in the Resistance, didn't hesitate to chuck a camembert at the head of an officer whom he thought had given a totally stupid order — a gesture that, it is easy to guess, was not without its consequences.

And now here he was, with his nose in the air, trying to

find his father's flag among those pitiable trophies that in times gone by made the ideal target for the enemy gunners but were no protection for the poor wretch who had to carry them. They were attached to the wall several yards above the floor, as tightly packed as lengths of material in a general store. The only way he could identify them was by the faded fragments of letters and badges hidden in their folds and almost impossible to decipher among all their golds, blues, and purples. His head thrown back, one after the other he passed them in review, progressing slowly, subjecting them to a meticulous examination as if, by means of this inventory, he were trying to discover and bring home the Napoleonic ashes of his father. This uncomfortable position soon made him feel dizzy; he lowered his head, passed a hand through his white hair, automatically took the tube of aspirin out of his pocket, and, still swallowing a pill, came back and leaned on the railing where he drowned his disappointment in sorrowful contemplation of the tomb.

That evening, while we were having dinner at a brasserie near the hotel (where for four days running our menu never varied, because from the second night on the waiter greeted us with a friendly "The usual?" — which so committed us that we felt we couldn't ask for anything different), Father felt unwell. He hadn't said a word from the beginning of the meal. The episode at the Invalides had visibly fatigued him. There had been the long wait in the ticket line where, standing in the rain in his gray suit, his jacket collar turned up in a pathetic attempt to protect himself, shielding the flame of his lighter with the hollow of his hand when he lit his cigarettes, he hadn't wanted us to relieve him because we would have had to leave the shelter of a porch. And then the vain search for his father's flag. Back at the hotel he had said he wanted to rest for a while before we went out to dinner.

You have now come to the day after Christmas. There's a ladder propped up against the roof of the shed where the clothes are dried. Climbing over the sheets of corrugated iron, being careful only to step on the places supported by the rafters so as not to fall through, your father is pruning the branches of the neighbor's plum tree that had gotten caught up in the telephone wires. The top of the leafless tree is swaying in the wind. Our troubleshooter is freeing the wires that the storm now brewing would be most likely to cut. When he comes down from the roof, gripping the ladder with extreme caution, he says he doesn't feel very well. This rather surprises you, because the effort involved was nothing special for him. In comparison with the enormous work he had put into renovating the house and garden, this bit of pruning can only qualify as a minor maintenance job. You've seen him move mountains, or at least chunks of mountains, which he stockpiles at the bottom of the garden, and a little sawing shouldn't be enough to exhaust him. Nor should his fatigue be attributed to age: after all, he's only forty-one, even though with his prematurely white hair and the very fact that he is your father, you don't see him as a young man.

For some time you have known that he has been in pain, and has been stuffing himself with pills to alleviate it. Not that he hasn't sought advice. He has seen so many doctors you can't keep track of them, and in desperation he has even made an appointment for the next day with a chiropractor. This you discover with amazement many years later, glancing through his diary. And this posthumous written trace leaves you with the strange impression that on the day after his death he was still alive, and that his real death dates from the first blank page in his diary. You can't help thinking that with empirical methods this country healer might perhaps have saved him.

The most eminent specialists declared, basing their opinions on X rays, that his back pains were caused by the compression of his intervertebral discs. They therefore advised him to stop carrying anything heavy. But when it comes to suitcases, it's difficult to do otherwise. This would mean giving up his profession, which in any case he is thinking of doing, but he has postponed the improvements to the garden, for which he has collected those remarkable stones that are now hidden under the long grass. They'll have to wait until his back leaves him in peace.

In this hope, he now gets up a quarter of an hour earlier every morning and scrupulously performs a long series of the exercises he had to do at the specialist's and which he wrote down in order to remember them. Lying on the bedside mat, his open notebook on the floor within reach, he puts himself through a succession of scissors movements, of body bends where he has to lean over and touch his toes, which isn't made any easier because he's so tall that his arms are short (his shirtsleeves all have a tuck in them at biceps level), exercises of this sort make him feel he's on his last legs, and anyway he doubts whether they're going to restore his worn-out discs. But at least if there isn't any improvement it won't be his fault.

His suffering isolates him. On Sundays, there's no longer any question of family outings. On the morning of his day of rest he stays in bed and, when he does get up, after his gymnastics all he does is hold his head in his hands and listen to the same records he's been putting on for months. Naturally, he had made the record player himself: he had been content to buy a motor unit and a turntable, and had made the casing out of plywood that he covered with adhesive plastic material, green imitation leather on the outside, and gray imitation marble on the inside. The loudspeaker is inside the radio. He is forever putting on his favorite group; they are a bit like an adult version of a boys' choir, only there aren't so many of them; that is, there's a soloist with a light, well-placed voice, who never seems to force the high notes, and eight other singers who mainly contribute to the choruses, in which they have to imitate the sound of bells or something of the sort. This probably has something to do with his lacking camaraderie and group solidarity. The football team, the theater company, the reunion of the "forty-year-olds" — these always end with songs. Perhaps, without realizing it, he identifies himself with the lead singer? "Joseph, if you'd seen him on the stage — he could just as well have become an actor." How many regrets is his reverie tinged with?

He is alone in a corner of the kitchen, listening to his records. He has moved a chair over by the record player, his cigarettes, lighter, and ashtray within reach on a little shelf. When he especially enjoys a song he immediately plays it again, lifting the arm and moving it back to the beginning very carefully so as not to scratch the disk. The shop doorbell, fixed just above the record player, adds a strident note to the choruses. He keeps putting off the moment of going to church, although the bell summoning the faithful to eleven o'clock Mass rang a long time ago. This lack of assiduity may well have more deep-seated reasons. He has recently confided his doubts to the curé

and, in quite a different vein from his usual menacing
sermons, Father Bideau has told him that even the greatest
mystics experienced these torments of the dark night of the
soul. It is flattering to be placed in such company, but for
the only faith that matters, the simple faith of the common
man, it's not a lot of help. And as an illustration of this
flaw, Bideau was to turn up too late to give him the last
rites.

As soon as he'd put the ladder and the saw away and
taken the branches he'd pruned into his workshop, intend-
ing to cut them up later, he told us he was going upstairs to
lie down. This is such an unusual occurrence in the middle
of the afternoon that you are asked not to make so much
noise — Your father's tired — since the kitchen where
you're playing is just underneath his bedroom. So you sit at
a corner of the table and draw, or start a game of cards in
silence. You don't suspect, though, that this is the beginning
of a kind of vigil. On New Year's Day, Mathilde, Cousin
Rémi's mother — they live together next door; their house
adjoins ours — confessed rather shamefacedly, almost
apologetically, as if she were making the unthinkable
worse, that she had attributed his indisposition to the previous day's chocolates.

In the evening, when it's dinnertime, he doesn't come
down but stays in bed. He probably drank the soup that
was taken up to him, or maybe he said he didn't want
anything. In which case you let him go on resting. You don't
see him again until you yourself are going up to bed. It must
be about ten o'clock and you go into his room timidly to
kiss him good night. You don't notice anything special: it's
just your father in his pajamas, his back supported by the
pillows, reading in the cone of light coming from his bedside lamp. It's a familiar sight — what is there in it to give

you cause for alarm? As the next day, December 27, is the feast of Saint-Jean l'Evangéliste, Saint John the Divine, he doesn't forget, as he kisses you, to wish you a happy name day. This man frightens you a little, even though he has never lifted a hand against you, but his authority is imposing and often renders you silent. So what are you going to feel when you hear, years later, that the reason he wanted you to be christened Jean was because that was the name of the beloved disciple whose feast day falls on that date? And anyway, you too are attached to the name and you never fail to protest whenever someone mixes him up with the other Jean, the twenty-fourth of June one, John the Baptist, the one who got beheaded. Much later still it will occur to you that it was also Saint John the Divine, the favorite, who recorded, "This is the disciple which testifieth of these things, and wrote these things."

Sometimes you'll find yourself telling people that his last words to you were to wish you a happy name day. Not so much because you want to improve on the truth ("and we know that his testimony is true"), but because it is an end that doesn't gain much by the coda that consists, at your mother's request no doubt, of taking him his lighter. Unless you did it on your own initiative. Because you don't really know how to approach this transitory father, you sometimes hope that doing this or that might get you in his good graces. So you go back to his bedroom, still timidly, and it isn't his illness that occasions your prudence — it's increased by the fear he inspires in you, which makes it difficult for you to act spontaneously.

You put the lighter down on the bedside table, hoping it will earn you a good mark in the form of that smile, which, now that you've tracked it down in his photographs, you can clearly see was characterized by kindness. It doesn't occur to you that the fact that he hasn't had a cigarette since the middle of the afternoon could be interpreted as a worrying sign. And anyway, he had several times declared he was going to give up smoking. Because the doctor had advised it? That would be a pity for the lighter, a fortieth-birthday present, a stainless steel lighter with a little toothed wheel on one side and a knob on top that releases the gas when you press it — a simultaneous double operation for which you need both hands. However many times your father explains how it works, showing you where to put your thumb and forefinger, cupping your hand in his, the lighter remains one of those Rubicon objects that demarcate the territory of childhood.

He thanks you. This time, these really are his last words. All you will ever hear from him now is a dreadful death rattle, dwindling as the minutes go by, when he is lying on the bathroom floor and entering his mortal agony.

You go back to your room. You slide under the two blankets and the bulky goose-feather eiderdown, kicking the scalding rubber hot-water bottle to the bottom of the bed. In its flannelette cover, it has been put there before bedtime and warmed the sheets while it was waiting for you. Outside, the wind is increasing to gale force and making the metal shop sign creak, as well as the advertising board of the nearby service station, hanging on its chains from the crosier at the top of a pole. Merged with these moans is the clatter of the slates being blasted off the roofs and smashing down below. Or it's some unknown object coming charging down the village street with the violent wind on its tail, or a shutter flapping, a bench being overturned, or a flowerpot jumping off a first floor window ledge without a safety net. The Lower Loire is accustomed to these sudden changes of mood, which soothe rather than disturb your slumbers.

Nice and safe, nice and warm, you're reading *Le Colonel Chabert*. Given the jacket, with its illustration of a knight by Géricault, it was certainly an abridged version for children, but when you wonder whether you were a precocious reader, you will remember that there was a more pressing reason than boredom for your having stopped reading a Balzac novel on the day after Christmas when you were eleven years old. In the next room — the connecting door is kept permanently open to let the warm air circulate more easily — your sisters are also reading. The bedtime chatter has stopped and is now replaced by the rustle of the pages being turned as a prelude to sleep. Suddenly, drowning the pandemonium of the storm, a muffled sound, this time from inside the house, jerks you out of your reading, it sounds as if a heavy body has fallen, and it's immediately followed by a startled cry coming from your mother. You scramble out of bed and rush over to the bathroom. You try to push the door open, but there's an obstacle on the other side, you try harder, but your mother, almost screaming, tells you to go around the other way. You pass through their bedroom, which is lit only by the bedside lamps so three quarters of it is in semidarkness. The double bed is empty, its blankets pushed back. In the adjoining bathroom, with its crude neon lighting, you find your father lying on his back on the gray linoleum, his eyes closed, his mouth open, his legs blocking the door to the landing. He is breathing heavily, raucously, as if there was an obstruction in his throat. Bending over his tall, dying body, your mother grips him by the shoulders, tries to sit him up, then takes his inert face in her hands. He had felt unwell — quick, we must call the doctor — he had tried to stand up — in the mirror over the sink she had seen his face suddenly become contorted, and just as she was about to rush over to him she had seen his body collapse backward. The fall, the floor shaking, the doctor, call him quickly, he hit his head against the wall as he fell.

Nina, the eldest, takes it upon herself to telephone. In vain. The line seems to be out of order. The storm. Then your mother drums on your bedroom wall, calling your cousin Rémi, who sleeps on the other side, to come and help. She is shouting and crying, still hammering on the wall with her fists. Rémi hears her and opens his window. After a frenzied exchange of words that are immediately snatched away by the wind, Mathilde, who has joined him and is also leaning out the window wearing a net over her white hair, says she'll run and fetch Dr. Maubrilland. Swathed in her dressing gown, with one of Rémi's jackets thrown over her shoulders — in her haste she grabbed the first thing that came to hand — her head in a scarf securely knotted under her chin, she dashes out into the gale, with slates flying all around her before they shatter on the ground, bent double against the wind, the sides of her dressing gown flapping like the wings of a birdman. In the meantime, Rémi runs to alert Aunt Marie in her dollhouse; that is, he runs as best he can, hobbling along with his lame leg, which he seems to have to drag out of the uneven ground with every step he takes. Soon they both come in from the garden, Aunt in the lead with her hurried little gait, her black coat over her nightgown, and the moment they get through the door the whole village is plunged into darkness. Rémi has his windproof lighter, with which he regularly warms the tip of his nose when he's relighting his hand-rolled cornsilk cigarettes for the twentieth time. In his beautiful strong voice, which qualifies him to be chief chorister at the great liturgical ceremonies, he tells the household not to worry, he knows where the oil lamps are kept. He does know, but only vaguely, it would seem, judging by the commotion in the cupboard. He asks Marie to bring him a chair so he can reach the top shelf, tells her to hurry up because he's burning himself with his blowtorch-lighter. An exasperated little argument in an undertone. Soon, a faint glimmer of light makes its way up the stairwell. Your mother goes down to meet the savior. In the halo of his lamp, Rémi catches sight of her poor, scared face, and with an affectionate gesture puts his free hand on the future young widow's shoulder. "The doctor will be here in a minute," he says.

But he wasn't. Since his bell isn't working, Mathilde throws stones at the doctor's windows, but he doesn't hear because his bedroom is on the garden side. Or he doesn't want to hear. For a long time afterward you will suspect him of having turned a deaf ear when he claims in his defense that he had attributed the machine-gunning of his windows to the storm. In the meantime, Rémi has put an oil lamp on the chest of drawers in the bathroom as near as possible to the body, whose death rattle is now gradually subsiding. Your Aunt Marie takes all three of you into the larger of the two bedrooms overlooking the street. Your sisters' books are still open on the bed at the fateful page. The feeble flame of the candle in its red ceramic holder on the bedside table doesn't throw any light on the complex structure of stovepipes comprising the ingenious paternal heating system. So when she goes over to the window to watch for Mathilde, your little aunt is most surprised to bump her forehead hard against a pipe running diagonally; being so pocket-size she's not used to having to lower her head. Half stunned, she mumbles "Joseph," but you don't know whether she's grumbling about his talents as an inventor or calling him to help her. Even if Joseph has heard her, he has only just enough breath left to make a little circle of mist on the mirror held in front of his mouth. When she's made sure that the great tubular contraption doesn't look likely to collapse, still rubbing her forehead she gives each of you a rosary. Her rosaries — her pockets are full of them and they get tangled up in her handkerchiefs — are of the austere type: black beads with silvery links. She casts a disapproving eye on the three of you huddling together in the same bed as she falls on her knees on the mat beside it, her knee joints cracking, her arms outstretched, her head raised up to the heavens (that is to say, the ceiling), her eyelids lowered, before starting, with your participation, on a kind of prayer marathon: "Our Father who art in heaven hallowed be thy name," followed by "Hail Mary full of grace the Lord is with thee" recited ten times, then back to Our Father followed by another ten Aves (which makes the woman's place ten times as important), the rhythm accelerating as her rosary revolves, so that you lose count and are rewarded with an irritated remark when you get out of time and recite an Ave when it should have been a Pater.

You hear steps on the landing, and a commotion that you imagine means the doctor has finally arrived. Mathilde puts her head through the door to confirm this. As a result your little aunt steps up the pace, as if she had decided to unite her forces with those of the professional to engage in the final battle. She invites Mathilde to join your group, and then Rémi, who has come to see how you are. Both, though, consider that they'll be more useful if they stay with your mother. But this is the sort of rational argument that carries no weight with your Marie. She is so convinced of the power of prayer that she would almost be prepared to hold them both responsible if by any chance things were to turn out badly. So then, to make up for the disastrous effect of this desertion, she raises her voice and you soon reap the benefit of this intense spiritual activity: the lights come back on. You leave the candle burning, however, fearing a further cut, even though it looks as if the storm is beginning to subside. Encouraged by this first victory, the little aunt makes a spurt, and this time you get completely lost, quite incapable of keeping up with the whirling dervish speed at which she's spinning her rosary. You let her carry on with her long-distance invocation on her own, sustained by the heavenly powers and the hope of salvation. Although the bed is so high that her crumpled little face is only just visible over the mattress, she seems to you to be levitating; so much so that you dart a quick glance to check that her knees haven't left the ground. Lulled by the monotonous rhythm of the prayers, you gradually fall asleep. You wouldn't be able to say how much time has passed since the tragic fall when someone, you've forgotten who, pushes the bedroom door open and, after a silence, simply announces: It's over.

This is a vague expression and could be adapted to a thousand situations. And yet you spontaneously understand that on this twenty-sixth of December nineteen hundred and sixty-three, at the age of forty-one, your father has just died.

II

*H*E WAS CERTAINLY one of those people who had the least to lose, except his life, but you wondered whether he really cared so much about his life when you remembered All Saints' Day 1941 and the tall, sad young man in the mourning overcoat leaning over his family grave, incapable of tearing himself away from the magnetic power of the granite tombstone on which the names of his parents were carved on either side of the recumbent cross, together with the guillotine-blade dates of his recent misfortune. Fifteen months had gone by since then, during which he had learned to live alone with his dark memories, when one February morning, on his twenty-first birthday, he received a notification from the Nantes Prefecture informing him that an official committee had detailed him for forced labor in Germany. This was a recent measure. He was one of the very first to benefit from it. Their factories were shorthanded, since their workers had been called up to close the gaps on all fronts, so the German authorities had invited the Vichy government to "compile a register of Frenchmen whose work was not of national importance." The same committee had decided that one person who answered this description was the sad young man who, without any great enthusiasm but because the times didn't have much to offer and you have to live, was now running the little shop inherited from his parents, which the village could certainly do without.

As if listing a schoolboy's outfit, the letter specified that he had to take with him: warm clothing, shoes both for "heavy duty" and for "best," enough provisions for a

two-day journey, and the three photographs necessary for a
passport. To all this he added as many books as his suitcase
could hold, among them *The Three Musketeers,* an adaptation of which he had staged during this last bleak year. A
very free adaptation, on the lines of the plays based on
popular novels that the little company of friends had put on
over the last few years for their own amusement: *The Mys-
teries of Paris, The Hunchback, The Count of Monte
Cristo,* and an unforgettable (for those who saw it, and are
still talking about it) pastiche of Jules Verne entitled
Around the Stage in Eighty Minutes, with a whole lot of
complicated machinery — balloon basket soaring up into
the flies, magic carpet, trapdoors, disappearing acts, apparitions, backdrops — plus a cardboard elephant and a live
camel that the group of friends had gone to fetch from La
Baule, where in the summer it roams the long sandy beach
giving rides to children and grown-ups, and during the rest
of the year vegetates in a garage. They brought it back in
triumph, on foot, and the crowd milling around on the
night of the performance welcomed it as the star of the
occasion, a reception that the great blasé camel greeted with
a disdainful sneer.

When he had announced that he was going to stage the
Dumas book, his friends imagined that he would cast himself as d'Artagnan, or at least as one of the three musketeers, but he told them that if they didn't mind he would
rather be Planchet, the servant, a part he wanted to play for
laughs. The project was well advanced, the rehearsals in the
parish hall were coming to an end, and the date of the first
night (which was only ever intended to be followed by a
second, or at the very most a third) was fixed. This departure for Germany was most unfortunate, but how could it
be avoided when the missive threatened reprisals in case of

defection or evasive action — reprisals that the fate of the
fusillés de Châteaubriant compelled you to take seriously.
There were only two members of his family left now. His
cousin Rémi, with his game leg, didn't have much to fear,
and what was more he was a war orphan, but there was also
Aunt Marie, his companion in grief who, since she had been
wearing mourning for the last twenty-five years, hadn't had
to make any changes in her meager wardrobe when her last
brother died. He was the only one of the three who had
come back alive from the agony of the 1914 war, and a few
months after the death of his wife he had permanently laid
down his arms and let himself die of a broken heart.

And now they were taking her nephew from her. And
while she is helping with the preparations for his departure,
she expresses her surprise that instead of returning his ration coupons as required by the letter, he has tucked them
into the lining of his jacket. But his only reply is to give her
his last instructions about the house (she is to live in it), the
shop (she is to open it in her spare time, if her teaching
duties allow her any, until all the stocks have been sold),
and the theater. Because right from the start he had enrolled
her in the little company and, flattered that he needed her,
she had allowed herself to be persuaded. Not to play the
duennas. She found her place at stage level, in the prompter's box. After their day's work, the apprentice actors —
butchers, charcutiers, cobblers, carpenters, roofers, plumb-
ers, grocers — sometimes found it difficult to learn and
remember their lines. Naturally, the parts were as far as
possible cast in accordance with their individual talents, but
Aunt Marie is the indispensable coordinator between the
fellow who takes himself for the actor Jules Berry and
reinvents his lines and the one who is capable only of
mumbling his way through his bits of dialogue. She stops

them from going astray, she brings the ones who get lost back on the straight and narrow, and in her best irritated-schoolmistress tone, she scolds the naughty pupils who have forgotten what they had learned. Since they have all been her pupils and remember how angry she can get, the occasional actresses have gotten their parts down pat and know them much better than the young men, which strengthens her in her conviction of the excellence of her method and encourages her to launch her little prefeminist speech, already delivered a thousand times, about the serious-mindedness of girls and their greater maturity, a speech that could also be understood as a defense and illustration of her celibacy.

On the evening of the first night she was at her post down in her sentry box, having arrived at the theater well before everyone else, all the more concerned that the show should run smoothly because Joseph had handed over the reins to her. She had presided over the last rehearsals as if she were the guardian of the temple, cutting short the au-tonomistic vagaries of the village Jules Berry and urging the rest of the company to respect both the letter and the spirit of her nephew's work. On his recommendation, for lack of an adequate last-minute stand-in she has turned Planchet into a kind of mute moron and given the part to the gar-dener at the girls' school. This worthy had no difficulty in adapting to his new function, as stomach rumblings were his natural form of expression — so much so that she had to act as his interpreter to his fellow actors. She had ex-plained that all he had to do was follow d'Artagnan like his shadow when asked to do so and to answer his questions with a grunt. Did he understand? He grunted. He had just passed his audition with honors.

The hall was full. A few German uniforms were to be seen in the audience. They had arrived one sunny Sunday in July 1940 as the congregation was just coming out of eleven o'clock Mass. The faithful had been standing in the square outside the church, discussing the enemy advance — some people had good news: they'd been halted at Saumur — when a couple of spluttering motorbikes came charging up the village street, effected a perfectly controlled skid, and stopped in front of the main entrance to the church. At the sight of their getup, which made it look as if motorbike and motorbiker formed a single unit that had been dipped into a gray-green sauce, even the least intelligent of the onlookers realized that the Saumur plug had been pulled. And while the man in the sidecar, helmeted and begoggled, was aiming his submachine gun at the parishioners, Maryvonne was heard to sigh "That's all we needed," which subsequently was unanimously acclaimed as Random's first act of resistance.

The second was to be credited to the rural policeman who every Sunday at that hour rounded up the population by beating his drum and then reading aloud the various announcements relating to the life of the village. This unexpected arrival just as he was making his appearance seemed likely to ruin his regular Sunday number, all the more so since the bikers had in the meantime been joined by a cohort of cars and covered trucks, crammed full of men at arms, which had surrounded the square. With his drum slung over his shoulder he advanced toward the officer commanding the detachment, clicked his heels — which didn't make much of a noise in comparison with the German jackboots — and, saluting, stated his grievances. As an officer himself, only a municipal one, true, but nevertheless a sworn official, it was his duty to inform the citizens of the latest communal decrees. What? What had he said that was so funny? A few words pronounced by the German officer in his own language had been enough to spread instantaneous mirth among the entire soldiery. The natives, however, couldn't see that there was anything to laugh at. Correct, the occupiers? Presumptuous, rather (they even wanted to invite themselves into the homes of the villagers), and obviously lacking in tact. They had never been so humiliated. This was when the rural policeman saw fit to pull his drumsticks out of the diagonal straps across his chest, to take them in his hands in the correct manner (a different hold for the left and the right hand), and while retreating with circumspection, like a trial run, a surreptitious rehearsal, beat out a short, rhythmical message: ta tataratata, which, according to the version he gave later, was supposed to represent the *"Tiens voilà du boudin"* in the coarse language of the Foreign Legion, but which other people, perhaps to justify themselves for having lost their nerve, more meanly attributed to the fact that his hands were trembling.

Now, when the heavy red curtain went up after the traditional three knocks, he was there in the middle of the stage with his avenging drum. It was only his uniform that had changed: it now transported the audience three centuries into the past, to the time of Richelieu's cats. All the little seamstresses in Random had donated their time and talents, ransacked their attics, and salvaged the slipcovers from discarded chairs and the lace from old-fashioned dresses. Reconstituted, the illusion of velvet and guipure was complete. Behind the rural policeman, now transformed into a herald in his cardboard boots with their wide turn-downs and his battered felt hunting hat adorned with

cocks' feathers, was a backdrop painted in ochers and pinks
that represented something like the Place des Vosges in
trompe l'oeil — for the near-sighted, at least. Descending
from the flies on a couple of ropes was the pediment of a
porch on which a station signboard announced MEUNG-
SUR-LOIRE, which merely had to be altered according to the
place changes, which, given the geographical complexity of
the story, allowed the action to move on from one scene to
the next, as the decor of the rechristened square stood for
every other square. The props were minimal: stage left, a
horse trough; stage right, an inn table with wooden benches
around it and above it an imitation wrought-iron inn sign:
HÔTEL DU FRANC MEUNIER. Opinions were already divided
in the audience, and subdued murmurs began to be heard.
Was the "Franc" to be seen as the declaration of a claim to
their French identity under the very nose of the occupier,
and did the "Meunier" — the Miller — mean that the country was being put through the mill? Soon, though, a few
local scholars spread the word that no, no, it really is called
that in the novel. And anyway, after he had executed a
whole lot of rat-tat-tats and tried out some unprecedented
drum rolls, Louis XIII's rural policeman pulled a scroll out
of his game bag, untied its red ribbon, held it at arm's
length, and began to read: "Oyez, oyez, take notice! Any
resemblance to true facts and to characters now living or
who have previously lived is in no way attributable to the
adapters of this historic play, but to the true facts and to
characters now living or who have previously lived." There
followed a short introduction describing the young d'Artagnan's departure from his parents' house, armed with the
letter of introduction from his father to Monsieur de Tré-
ville, the captain of the king's musketeers. "And now, let the
show commence!" The rural policeman had taken it into his

head to dramatize his number by twirling his drumsticks in his fingers, but at the last rehearsal one of them had landed down in the prompter's box and our little aunt had come within an ace of having an eye gouged out, so she had decided that enough was enough.

Even when she was perched on two fat dictionaries, her eyes barely came up to the level of the boards. Clutching the edge of the stage, with the pages typed by her nephew spread out under her nose, she mouthed all the actors' dialogue as they spoke it. When one of them forgot his lines she made her voice heard in her own particular fashion — inherited from her years of practice of saying prayers and going to church — which was to speak loudly in a low voice, so that she could sometimes be heard by the audience, who now and then joined in in chorus as the actor spoke his words.

There were now three people on stage. Watched by a pretty blonde, the apprentice musketeer was clashing swords with a gentleman. Since the swords were made of wood, the director had asked his pal André to sharpen two big butcher's knives against each other in the wings. The success of this sound effect depended on perfect synchronization. It had been decided that they would exchange thirty thrusts. So as not to spoil his effect, the young man with the trembling hands, who already overindulged in wine, asked Aunt Marie to count with him. She was afraid of a thirty-first thrust, which would have ruined the scene but which didn't happen. Everything would have been perfect if André, who was playing the innkeeper, hadn't made his entrance carrying his knives — to the great delight of the audience.

In spite of its brocades and laces, Milady's green gown was not guaranteed to be of the correct period, but the palpitating young bosom swelling its décolleté was of a universal nature. A fact that didn't escape her fellow actors. Hidden in her prompter's box, our little aunt was keeping a weather eye open and casting an occasional glance over her spectacles. When the gentleman-carpenter got a little too close to the graceful young woman, she discreetly called him to order by tapping her pencil on the boards. In his departing instructions her nephew had made no allusion to it, but she was not unaware of the fact that the beautiful Milady was his unofficial fiancée.

She came from a nearby village. They had met at a wedding. In rural communities, wedding processions are the most efficacious of all matrimonial agencies. Both families take a lot of trouble in matching the couples. These two families had thought that the tall, sad, recently bereaved young man might find some sweet consolation in the beautiful, radiant sun taking his arm. At any rate, he had found his Milady in Emilienne.

Because the young starlet had absolutely no acting experience, an occasion presented itself for her to try out her talents in a Passion play put on in Random by the assistant priest. This was an unusual kind of exercise, closer to an Easter reading than to theater proper, but it had the advantage of entertaining the faithful while at the same time offering them an edifying spectacle. Nevertheless, the project came up against a veto from the bishop of Nantes, who had forbidden mixed performances ever since Saint Veronica had given birth to a child whose paternity was much disputed between the apostles in one of the communes in his diocese. This affair had created a great stir among the right-thinking. "THE RETURN OF SODOM" was the headline of one article in *Le Phare*, which then began: "When shall we see a Virgin Mary who has been made pregnant by her son?" The young assistant priest, who was far more frightened at the idea of the women being played by men in drag, leaped courageously to his own defense. He managed to get an appointment at the bishop's palace and pleaded his cause. "Again!" thundered the bishop, suddenly abandoning his preliminary unctuousness ("Well, so you're at Random. Do you like it? Good, good," all the time rubbing his hands in a circular movement. "And to what do I owe the pleasure of your visit?"). "No, no, NO! — you're at least the tenth person to ask me the same thing. No mixed performances of Passion plays." But the young abbé had not embarked on his appeal without due preparation: "No doubt, Monsignor, but have you considered the disastrous effect on our faithful, accustomed to the beautiful madonnas in our churches, of an imperfectly shaved Virgin, with hairy hands and size ten shoes?" His argument registered, and after a few objections that were soon swept aside, the bishop surrendered: "Very well, but in that case I will only allow you three women — the Virgin Mary, about fifty years old, which is to say the right age for the part [which reduced the risks], Mary Magdalene [no instructions; a sinner has to be allowed to sin], and the wife of Pontius Pilate." The abbé thanked his superior warmly and, while he was kissing the purple stone at the extremity of the arm stretched out toward him, vainly racked his brains to find any trace of a wife of Pilate he might have come across in his reading of the gospels. But that was how Emilienne inherited the nonspeaking role created by episcopal fantasy.

Dressed in a long white tunic girdled with a golden cord, she illuminated the Passion play with her presence. When she gave her husband the towel to dry his hands on, the men in the audience felt their palms grow moist. Their attention was so riveted on her golden tresses and her curves that the priest was the only one to tear his hair when Christ on the cross, in the center of the darkened stage, with only his face visible in the spotlights, suddenly declared in a voice full of conviction, as if he'd just finished a hard day's work in the fields, "I'm parrrched." It's true that there was nothing in that to shock an audience accustomed to speaking and hearing the local patois.

Previously unknown in Random, Emilienne was known from then on as "Pilate's wife," a pseudonym that stuck. This training in perfidy as the consort of the most famous of all lily-livered hygienists, reinforced a few months later by her character of Milady, would, it seemed, decide her fate. Jesus reincarnated as d'Artagnan (in both cases, the young farm worker had owed his role less to his acting talents than to his mop of wavy hair), had also been touched by grace. Speaking from the horse trough into which the gentleman had knocked him, he addressed the gentleman in scathing tones: "Monsieur, you are as cowardly as Madame is beautiful." Then, when he turned to the winsome lady, words failed him. "And vice versa," our aunt prompted him, which was supposed to mean "Madame, you are as beautiful as Monsieur is cowardly." But the flustered gallant could no longer marshal his thoughts. And, as the beauty was growing impatient, he addressed her in a mumble: "And vice versa," and then, blushing, pretended to faint.

Our little aunt probably raised her eyes to heaven, which, for her, came to the same thing as calling on God to witness her earthly woes, and then turned them anxiously toward the wings, from which Planchet was supposed to make his entrance. She had entrusted him with the job of changing two of the signboards: MEUNG-SUR-LOIRE to

PARIS, and HÔTEL DU FRANC MEUNIER to POMME DE PIN. Even though his role had been thoroughly slimmed down, the gardener had given her plenty of headaches during the final rehearsals. The most difficult thing had been to stop him from punctuating his grunts with long brown jets of spittle. Not that he was suffering from a blockage of the bronchial tubes, but he chewed tobacco and spat out his used quid into his beret, which never failed to intrigue the uninitiated. Maryvonne, the wardrobe mistress and makeup artist (she who never wore anything but overalls, and who contented herself with a little pink face powder on Sundays), had suggested that he might expectorate into a handkerchief, which she would embroider with his stage name. Such a tactful thought: he promised to try.

While the others, on the days before the performance, were conscientiously rehearsing their lines, the gardener would be practicing targeting his spittle into a crumpled square of cloth held in the hollow of his hand. The latest news was that his aim was accurate, but our little aunt, with her nose at stage level, was always afraid of being hit by the spray. Her anxiety grew even greater when she discovered that Planchet, who had just entered, had in the meantime grown a whole head taller. He was wearing a tow wig, his outrageously rouged cheekbones made him look like a clown, but that great height, that way of imitating the humble valet, gauche and servile, ever ready to bow down to the ground . . . "Joseph, is that you?" she said. And the docile Planchet repeated, "Joseph, is that you?" The darkened murmurs coming from the other side of the footlights suddenly gave way to silence. Judging by the voice, there was no longer any doubt. "Joseph, you're mad." He repeated, "Joseph, you're mad." A stupefied "Oh!" rippled through every row. "Joseph, be careful, there are Germans here." And he, addressing the audience, "The Cardinal's spies — here?" All heads anxiously turned toward the German soldiers. However, not understanding the language, they obviously didn't realize what was going on, and the audience began to chuckle. The murmurs grew louder, laughs rang out, and a wave of applause greeted the intrepid revenant. A few scenes later, the theater was in an uproar. Just as d'Artagnan was setting sail for England to recover the queen's diamond studs, Planchet came rushing in brandishing two fishing rods. "I'm taking *deux gaules*," he announced. The house went wild, and as the two companions-in-arms, perched on a little cardboard boat, were crossing the stage against the background of a raging sea, Planchet, as a figurehead, hoisted his two fishing rods as high as his arms could reach, where, against the blue of the backcloth sky, they formed an enormous V.

It was a triumph. But when the actors came on to take their bows, the hero of the evening had once again disappeared. The moment the curtain fell, our little aunt rushed backstage. "Where is he?" she asked Maryvonne. "Gone," replied the grocery lady, pointing to the stage door. Hadn't he left a message? Yes, this letter for Emilienne. But for his aunt, who was all the family he had, who was running his business, who had staged his play, and who worried herself sick about her nephew, nothing?

The young men were herded together on the station platform, surrounded by soldiers, waiting for the train that was to transport them to Germany. In spite of the mildness of this steely blue March morning, tempered by a chilly little wind enfilading the tracks, they were warmly equipped in preparation for the harsh climate they had been told to expect. Each man was dressed according to his condition in life, his overcoat more or less well fitting, more or less threadbare; the more humble of them had piled on as many clothes as possible under a tight little jacket whose buttons were feeling the strain. At their feet was a suitcase containing everything they had been ordered to bring with them: a change of clothes, of shoes, either "heavy duty" or "best" (depending on which pair they had put on that morning), and enough provisions to last over a long two-day journey. Some of them had added a knapsack that revealed the neck of a bottle of wine with its cork sticking out — a miraculous commodity in these difficult times. When they extracted their bottle and took a swig, the most swashbuckling among them would first belch, and then boast, "That's another one the Germans won't get," or "Like in 1914, it's wine that'll win the war," which in the circumstances raised no more than a half-hearted smile. Most of them remained silent, like on your first day in a new class at school when you don't yet know each other, when you're sizing each other up, hoping to see some signs of fellow feeling. When a distant hissing sound announced the arrival of a train, they turned their resigned faces toward the wide curve in the track around which the expected locomotive would suddenly appear in a cloud of steam.

The most ardent desire of the man who was a head taller than all the rest was to escape attention. This was the moment of truth. When the letter arrived he had known at once that this was not going to be the way he would discover Germany. And as he had had his call-up papers duly stamped, and therefore felt he no longer needed to worry about his aunt, what he had to do now was find some way of giving his companions the slip. Would he wait until he was on board and then jump from the moving train? Or could he manage to escape by unobtrusively sliding under the cars? He was bending over to glance under the train standing at the other platform when a suspicious soldier came up and pushed him back into the ranks with the barrel of his submachine gun. "Cigarette," he said, pointing to a butt opportunely thrown on the ballast, and he jumped down on the track, retrieved it, and immediately started smoking it with relish to prove his good faith. At least he had seen what he wanted to see. It was possible to creep under a car with his suitcase, and later emerge on the opposite platform — hoping to avoid any unpleasant surprises on that side. All he had to do now was wait for an auspicious moment, stepping back a few paces to try to merge into the crowd of his companions in adversity, coming to terms with his mounting fear, and answering one of the men who suggested making a dash for it by raising his eyebrows questioningly.

When, in a cacophony of connecting rods, pistons, brake shoes, and bursts of steam, the train slowly drew up at the platform, there was a mad rush for the doors in search of seats, since the young men leaning against the windows, having got in at Saint-Nazaire, had announced that there wouldn't be enough for everyone. While the sentries were fully occupied in restoring discipline by giving gruff orders, he slid down with his suitcase between two cars, worked his way beneath the couplings, and crept under the other train. Lying flat on his stomach across the railroad ties, his heart beating frantically, for an eternity of seconds he awaited the shouts and hysterical activity that would certainly ensue if his escape had been noticed. Every time a whistle blew to signal the departure of a train, he tightened his grip on his suitcase, ready to spring, reproaching himself for having loaded it down with so many books, although not for a single moment did it occur to him to abandon it. As the minutes passed and the normal frenzy of the occupants sounded no more alarming than usual, he began to crawl forward a few yards, all the time keeping a watch on the feet clomping along the platform above him. Even more than a pair of boots, what he dreaded to see were the four paws of a German shepherd, whose nose would certainly have condemned him, whose fangs would have torn him to pieces. But neither boots nor dog appeared. All that was to be seen through the narrow gap between the bottom of the carriage and the edge of the platform was the heartrending procession of miserable substitutes for shoes. Old, worn-out, patched-up shoes, complete with wooden or cork soles, or even with a bit of carpet. He himself, in preparation for his getaway, had made a deal with the postman, who got preferential treatment, and had acquired a pair of sturdy leather shoes. He had remembered a remark made by a prisoner who had escaped from a stalag: "The secret of an escape is shoes."

For the time being, though, a blacksmith's apron would probably have served his purpose better, as he made his way along under the train, bumping his suitcase over the ties in front of him. Another thing he feared was that the train above him would pull out. He could imagine the tragicomedy of the scene, with him on all fours in the middle of the rails, his pathetic surrender and its terrible consequences. What could he pretend to be looking for? The cigarette butt story wouldn't work a second time. But anyway, this was it, this was the end of his disappearing act: a slight jolt, an imperceptible gliding movement — though his temporary shelter hasn't budged. A comparison of the position of the wheels with a fixed point is enough to reassure him: it's the train transporting the forced laborers that is pulling out, on the other track. And he aims a relieved little smile at the ties and axles: the contingent bound for Germany is leaving without him.

By now he has reached the end car and, flat on his stomach, takes stock of the situation: cars waiting or abandoned on a siding, a railwayman pulling up a lever at the points, some workmen chatting by a shed, a contemplative seagull perched on a rail, sparrows hopping up and down. The track on this side crosses the west side of the town. If he were to walk along it, with that wire fence between the station and the avenue, he could hardly escape notice. Should he cut through the marshaling yard to get down to the river? Too many pitfalls, and he would be almost certain to come across a patrol. Wait until it gets dark? Without a secure hiding place, he wouldn't like to bet on his chances until then. All that remains is the station. And he leaves his cover, bending double as he crosses the rails, as if his great height made him too conspicuous, pausing, crouched down under the end of the platforms, risking a glance, but still squatting there on the lookout for the arrival of a train that would allow him to melt into the crowd of passengers. Dusting off his overcoat to improve his appearance, he notices that it has lost a couple of buttons, one of which has taken a bit of cloth with it. There are greasy patches that refuse to come off, and he even adds a bit of blood to them, which to his great surprise comes from his hand. While he is examining his wound, a few drops of rain fall on his open palm. He looks up. The sky has taken advantage of his sojourn undercover to muster up some dark, heavy rain clouds, which precipitate a splendid deluge. The master of the elements is generous: the rain, which reduces people's ardor, will be an invaluable ally. The watchdogs aren't going to look twice, being more interested in finding shelter.

The rain is now pelting down on all sides, creating a halo of vapor above the steaming locomotive, which has just appeared around the wide curve. It seems to be trying to find its way among the points, and then passes within a few inches of him, spitting sparks. He nimbly hoists himself up on the platform and is soon just one of a group of passengers. In spite of his fears, he doesn't stand out too much in his shabby getup. War doesn't make it any easier for people to buy new clothes, and some have great difficulty in disguising their destitution. He is even amused at the way the women have drawn a thin pencil line over their tea-tanned calves to simulate the seam of imaginary silk stockings. But his anxiety grows when he notices several people staring at him, as if his new condition of a man on the run had branded a star on his forehead. "I've had it," he says to himself, and he feels an icy liquid piercing his heart. He walks more slowly and, to keep up his courage, lights a cigarette. When the flame reflects his face in a train window, he realizes that what had caught their attention was the streak of black oil covering his nose. The very thing for daytime camouflage.

The exit toward which the crowd of passengers is moving is under strict surveillance. In view of the increasing number of assassination attempts and acts of sabotage, the German police, backed up by the recently created militia who, so it is rumored, are even more to be feared, have intensified their control with the frenzy of lost causes. For the tide is beginning to turn against the upholders of the new order. He can see them barring the exit, suspicious, touchy, irritable, impatient, checking papers, opening bags and suitcases, and for no apparent reason picking on one man, who casts a fearful glance around him, and pulling him to one side. Should he cut across to the station restaurant? He has to be on his guard against plainclothes policemen and informers who lean on the bar pretending to be unconcerned but then suddenly abandon their drinks and start following you. Arrests of this type, muttered conversations have reported, are the most pernicious, because they also affect the friend who is hiding you, and sometimes lead them to pick up a whole Resistance network. As he catches sight of the waiting room, he remembers a Latin translation from his school years where a crafty shepherd spirits away some oxen by pushing them out of a cave backward, which causes some incredulity in their owner, Hercules maybe, who is misled by their footprints. But that would mean passing the ticket collector in the opposite direction. So he goes up to him and, covered in confusion, putting on his Planchet act, explains that he doesn't know the time of his connection at Angers for Sablé, changing at, that's just it, he's forgotten where: could he possibly go back to the information office? "Make it quick, then," grumbles the official, irritated that he doesn't know the answers by heart.

In the waiting room, apart from the passengers actually waiting, there are quite a few passersby who, caught in the shower, have hurried in to dry, still out of breath from their little sprint, wringing out their hair and shaking their overcoats. Others, crowding into the doorway, are waiting for the sky to clear and indulging in inspired comments: "The English are at it again," someone hazards, while the rain buckets down even harder on the cobblestones.

The tall young man with the suitcase has worked his way into the front row, deaf to the protesters standing on tiptoe watching the vagaries of the sky over his shoulder. He shivers in the moist breeze brought by the shower and pulls his coat collar tighter around his neck. The stream flowing in front of him, a former branch of the Loire recently filled in to prevent spring floods, seems to have reverted to its original state. The running water glistens like a great river, froths up in the gutters, and rushes down the gratings into the drains. It is as if the rain has the deserted town at its mercy and has brought it to a standstill. The comments become rarer, more laconic, everyone is plunged into pleasant contemplation. A kind of inner peace is achieved. The tall young man has taken off his glasses and is rubbing the top of his nose. He can be seen to be of two minds about whether to put them on again but then slips them into his pocket. Why does he need to see clearly in this murky atmosphere? The haze that now surrounds him seems to keep danger at arm's length, to attenuate it, like the massive towers of Anne of Brittany's castle, which he can see in the distance through the mists. And, benefiting from what might be taken for blind confidence, the ultimate negligence, he suddenly dives out into the cover of the liquid canopy.

The kindly rain even makes it possible for him to walk more quickly without his haste appearing suspicious: after all, he is merely a simple pedestrian who refuses to submit to the dictates of the heavens. He is getting farther away from the danger zone, but he still doesn't allow himself to look over his shoulder, or give way to the delirium of joy overwhelming his final reservations. His sturdy shoes make a mockery of the puddles and seem like seven-league boots; his suitcase no longer weighs down his arm. He will have plenty of time to read, now, and he no longer regrets having filled it so full. At last he looks behind him. No one is following him. And, under the protection of the mighty ramparts of the ducal castle, he allows himself to take his first deep breath as a free man.

His friends would probably not be expecting him so soon. He was already savoring the moment when he would knock at their door, they would open it, and, with a mischievous grin, casually adjusting his glasses behind his ears, he would simply say to his astonished hosts, "I missed the train." He had planned his escape down to the last detail. All he had to do now was cut across to the harbor, walk along the Quai de la Fosse of ill repute, where sailors' bars were now operating in the basements of the charming but dilapidated old mansions, and climb to the Butte Sainte-Anne, where one of his old schoolfriends lived over his father's carpentry workshop. In the not so distant past, when he was a boarder at the Catholic school in Chantenay, one of the poor suburbs of Nantes, just a few steps away, he had many times benefited from the generous hospitality of the Christophes, who already had so many people to cater to that one extra didn't make the slightest difference. There were three generations under one roof, and his schoolfriend Michel was the eldest of twelve children. He suffered from being an only son, and when they put up a cot for him in the workshop he loved to feel part of this turbulent throng who seemed completely indifferent to material difficulties. The recipe was simple, even though it lacked variety. Madame Christophe, whose figure had become somewhat problematic after her repeated pregnancies, had no rival in praising in every possible way the virtues of the potato, which the family cultivated on a vast scale in their land allotment on the outskirts of the town. It was with her in mind that he had refused to return his ration card (as well as his tobacco card, but in this case he was thinking more of himself), although his call-up papers had demanded that he hand it in to the appropriate authority. He would give his hostess his weekly sheet of J3 food coupons, the special ones for young men over thirteen that entitled them to more liberal rations. She would start by exclaiming, "But Joseph, you'll need them yourself, you're only here for a few days," but he would have plenty of arguments to persuade her, and in the end she would accept them and confess that they would help to butter a few parsnips, although for a long time no one had been able to find either the one or the other. "Save bread," the wall posters adjured the populace, "cut it in thin slices and use all the crusts for soup" — as if the workers' families were in the habit of throwing away the leftovers.

During the day, he would join Michel and his father in the workshop, as he had always done when he visited them before. His talents as a cabinetmaker had become apparent very early. When he was only twelve he had turned his cradle into a small table, although he'd made a pretty good hash of it. Next he had made an armchair; it had massive curves, but its seat was too narrow because he had forgotten to include the thickness of its arms in his calculations. At sixteen he had taken some friends on board a long canoe he had made and christened the *Pourquoi-Pas?* in memory of Captain Charcot, which didn't evince any great optimism when you remember how its illustrious eponym had ended up, crushed to bits by the ice floe. This marked preference for working in wood was no doubt inherited from his wooden-clog-making ancestors, who had been established for centuries in the heart of the Forêt du Gâvre, from where the last of the line — his grandfather, whom he hadn't known — had emigrated to open a little shop in Random, which had developed into a wholesale business after he cut off one of his fingers, and it was to this fatal, unfinished, rough-hewn wooden clog, emerging from a chunk of wood like a kind of sacrificial chopping block, that our family owed its conversion to the porcelain business. But the tools of our mutilated ancestor's trade still hung in our workshop: the knives, chisels, and gouges with which Father had carved out the arms and back of his armchair.

Under the guidance of his hosts, the young autodidact had become a skilled worker. He had even developed his own speciality: staircases. These demand a combination of dexterity, knowledge, and improvisation: in some cases, no two steps are alike. He may even have dreamed for a moment of making them his career. On one of the false identity cards dating from his underground period, made out in the name of Joseph Vauclair, born in Lorient, Morbihan (the town had been demolished in the bombings so its records had disappeared), on February 22, 1925 (by making himself three years younger, he was no longer eligible for forced labor in Germany), his Profession was given as Carpenter. This was a tribute to his adopted family and an insurance against being caught red-handed as a manifest incompetent if some foxy investigator asked him out of the blue: What's a trying plane, a marking gauge, a molding plane? And if any such catechist, mistrustful of the tall young man's appearance, were to suspect him of having gained his knowledge purely from books, he would only have to show his hands, which had already been hardened by farm work. Since at the end of his two weeks with the Christophes, it had been arranged that he would go and lie low in the countryside, where people of all sorts ultimately came together: volunteers, recalcitrants, outcasts, members of the Maquis, black marketeers. In this way they partially agreed with the marshal, who wanted people to go back to the land, even if the nation in peril was in the event primarily interested in the peasants' larders and their conveniently isolated villages.

But in the meantime, between the carpenter's shop and the farm, he had planned a detour to Random to make an unexpected appearance and perform his own kind of impromptu, in comparison with which the famous "Indian trunk" disappearing act would be no more than a feeble illusion. While everyone believed he was a forced laborer in Germany, he would reappear on stage as Planchet and brandish his fishing rods under the very nose of the occupier, only to vanish again like a latter-day Judex, leaving the astonished spectators momentarily converted to the Resistance. Momentarily, because immediately after the war was over, those very same people lost no time in refusing to consider any of the candidates who had belonged to the Resistance, preferring to reelect the existing municipal councilmen who had written such charming letters to the marshal congratulating him on his action and exhorting him not to forget Random.

The Christophes had tried to dissuade him: "Joseph, *The Three Musketeers*, whether there's one more or one less, and no one even knows exactly how many they were, but in any case they can get on perfectly well without you. You'd be taking too many risks for nothing much." But the "nothing much" in question was also called Emilienne, and that's the kind of risk that for a twenty-year-old justifies certain extravagances.

He left Nantes by stealth and pedaled hard through the growing dusk, his suitcase fastened to the carrier, his fishing rods strapped to the crossbar. He rode without lights to avoid attracting attention — he had removed the red reflector from the rear mudguard — diving behind a hedge with his bike every time some vehicle's headlights pierced the darkness — with a curfew in force, it could only be someone undesirable — stopping at a signpost to read it by the flame of his lighter since he had taken so many detours that he had finally gotten completely lost, arriving just as the show was about to begin, sneaking into the wings where while awaiting his entrance he put on his makeup and borrowed the poor gardener's wig, promising to give it back before the end of the show, which he did immediately after the scene of the embarcation for England. For this was no time to hang around. He wouldn't wait for the reward of his brilliant feat. And yet with what enthusiasm the company would have welcomed its hero. But the alarm might already have been raised. When he confided to Maryvonne, as he gave her a letter to pass on to the proper quarter, that he intended to call at the house to collect a few things and some more books, she told him that the Germans had commandeered his aunt's little cottage and that she, as he had requested, was camping in the big house with a group of students she had taken in as boarders so that any authoritarian squatters would come up against what might be seen as a "No Vacancies" sign. Three of these would-be squatters, kept at a respectful distance by this obstinate little force, had had to squeeze into the tiny little hermitage in the garden. So he abandoned his plan and set off once again on the road to Riancé. For a few kilometers he was seized with remorse at not having spared a little time for his courageous aunt. Why hadn't he at least left her a note? She, the ever-faithful, betrayed by her swaggerer of a nephew. All at once he felt less proud of himself. Soon it began to rain, a fine, insidious rain that, together with the coldness of the night, obliged him to look for shelter. He was far enough away, now. He spotted a barn, hid his bike, and went and curled up in the hay where, tired out, he fell asleep.

Very early the next morning he got off his bike outside the shop of Monsieur Burgaud, ladies' and gentlemen's tailor at Riancé, a firm founded in 1830 according to the aristocratic gilded coat of arms above the shop window. While waiting for the shop to open, he did his best to make himself presentable, extracting bits of hay from his clothes, wiping the lenses of his glasses, and running a comb through his hair, hoping for the best. Two girls passed him, giggling. They walked through the garden around to the back of the house and shortly afterward one of them began to crank up the shop shutter, once again looking curiously at the half-frozen young man rubbing his hands and stamping his feet on the pavement outside. Since there weren't any customers, he pushed the door open, and the little copper rods hanging above his head began to jingle. He was immediately enveloped in a warm smell of cloth, which consoled him for his night of vagrancy. The small glass window of the stove cast a flickering orange gleam on the floor. He was scrutinizing the piled-up lengths of cloth wound around their boards, admiring as a connoisseur the long, ornate counter with the square-sectioned wooden measure lying on it, when a woman came in from the back of the shop. By her slightly lopsided gait, which corresponded to the description he had been given of her, he recognized her as Madame Burgaud. "What can I do for you, Monsieur?" she asked suspiciously, keeping her distance from the tall young man who stank of hay. A lot, but he thought it would be more seemly to begin by introducing himself. No doubt she knew all about it — he had been sent by her daughter Marthe and her son-in-law Etienne, who, when they were first married a few years before the war, had gone to live in Random and taken over a firm dealing in grain.

It was Etienne, in whom he had confided after he received his call-up papers, who had advised him to go to Riancé. For the best of all reasons: you never saw a single German there. And then, another advantage in these days of shortages, the town was surrounded by forests that abounded in game, all the more so in that shooting was forbidden, so the most princely supplementary rations were available. Poaching was rife, and on some Sundays it wasn't unusual for venison to be served at the Burgauds' table. And anyway, since life in Random had become too difficult, that was where Etienne had sent his wife and three children. There was a warm welcome to be found at the house of his parents-in-law. Alphonse Burgaud knew all the peasants in the region, having at one time or another made suits for them — either for a funeral or a wedding — and he would certainly be able to find a farm willing to harbor the fugitive.

Madame Burgaud asked the tall young man to follow her, took him into the living room–dining room, invited him to sit down in spite of her fears that the tenacious smell of hay might contaminate her armchair, and went to fetch her husband. Three steps inlaid with mosaic led up to this room, which occupied a wing recently built on to the house. Lighted by large picture windows at an angle to each other, it looked out on a little enclosure where a tiny goat was prancing around untethered. Coming back unexpectedly, Madame Burgaud anticipated the question of the young man looking pensively out of the window and, pointing at the animal, said, "With his very unusual business sense, my husband is going to turn us all into goats."

As the peasants were short of liquid assets, the tradition being that money only came in at the end of the harvest —

and a suit sometimes didn't have the patience to wait —
Alphonse Burgaud accepted without haggling whatever he
was offered in exchange for his work. A goat for the biggest
jobs, some butter and eggs for the more modest ones, and
even "You can pay me next time," if his debtors were too
hard up. The first kid of a long and already ancient line of
descendants ended up on his table. When the three little
girls of the family, from whom the truth had been concealed, recognized in various roasts their playmate of the
last few weeks that had inexplicably disappeared, they began to sniffle, then great big tears fell on their plates, and
soon, in a chorus of sobs, they refused to touch their food,
whereupon Alphonse declared that he wasn't hungry either.
At which Claire, his wife, since that was the way it was,
grabbed the dish and tipped all its contents, plop, into the
garbage. The goats that followed — there had been as
many as four in the fenced enclosure in which there was a
log cabin — were allowed to take their time to grow up and
die a natural death, to the great displeasure of Claire, who
asked her husband to bring them to her as single compo-
nents in future. In spite of its size, it was a long time since
the last one had been a kid. A pituitary deficiency, no doubt,
but whatever it was it had allowed the peasant to drive a
hard bargain, because, honestly, all those yards of organdy,
those dozens of hours spent in plying the needle and ruining
one's eyesight, those long fitting sessions to ensure that the
bride would finally look like a fluffy little cloud — all this
was worth more than a dwarf goat.

The moment he came into the room, very dapper in a three-piece suit, his pepper-and-salt hair closely cropped, his mustache Chaplinesque, Alphonse Burgaud recognized his visitor and went up to him with outstretched hand. It had been just over two years ago, the sky was as gray as it should be on All Saints' Day, when the tailor had gone with his daughter Marthe to the cemetery in Random to visit the grave of her firstborn son, a short-lived little Jean-Clair. As he was making his way along a side path arm in arm with his daughter, he had noticed a tall young man in glasses supporting his forlorn father in front of a tombstone covered in flowers. From the abundance of flowers it was easy to guess the recent date of the tragic event, and from the prostration of the father, the magnitude of his grief. A year later, at the same memorial pilgrimage, the same tall young man was there alone. Bending over his family tombstone, he looked as if he was about to lie down on it. The prostrate father, overwhelmed by the intensity of his sorrow, had wasted no time in joining his wife under the gray granite tombstone, demonstrating by his haste a disconcerting fidelity from which he seemed to exclude the young man who, after all, had been the incarnation of his love. And now it was the turn of the abandoned son to weigh the idea of joining them, of resuming the warm place between father and mother of the miraculous child he had been — miraculous in that he had lived, after a long succession of stillborn babies. And that was the moment when Alphonse Burgaud had witnessed a kind of life-saving operation: a little white-haired lady, dressed all in black, her head sunk between her shoulders — an aunt, the most extraordinary schoolteacher in the Lower Loire department, if Marthe was to be believed — trotted up to the despairing young man, tugged at the young man's coat, rescued him from the hypnotic power of the recumbent stone, finally prevailed, and went off with him along the central path toward the cemetery gates.

By a strange quirk of fate, it was into his hands that this tall young man was now entrusting his safety, as if, pursued on all sides, he no longer knew what to do with the life he had so miraculously been granted. From the moment Etienne had appealed to him to play a part in this saga, which had already fascinated him as an onlooker, Alphonse Burgaud had started looking for a farm where the rebel could be hidden. He had found one at the edge of the forest, on the estate of the Count de la Brègne, the head of one of the most ancient families in France, which is to say neither more nor less ancient than any other but one that was able to trace the continuity of its name throughout the centuries, or at any rate to trace its zigzagging reputation back to an origin that distance rendered more prestigious, and which prompted a marchioness of the ancien régime, contesting the titles of a general of the empire, prince of this and duke of that, to say to him, "Yes, but *you* have no ancestors." To which the general, just as covered in glory and in wounds as the lowborn crusader who had been the founding father of her noble line, had magnificently replied, "But Madame — *we* are the ancestors." Although this wasn't very kind to his father, either, who may have been a simple innkeeper, a caste that has no pretentions to ancient lineage, unless of course among innkeepers themselves.

The Riancé tailor was made welcome at the castle. All he was required to do was turn up with his professional expertise and his sewing kit, because the Count had his suit fabric specially sent from the Shetland Islands. This greatly impressed Alphonse Burgaud, whose apprentice years with Paris couturiers had taught him to appreciate fine cloth and light, comfortable materials, such as a particular cashmere overcoat whose virtues he demonstrated by feeling its weight with his little finger. Taking for granted the Count's affinities with the British, he had at first intended to inform him that his tenant farmers might perhaps soon be called upon to harbor a defaulter from the forced labor system. But after the Count had made a few disagreeable remarks about a certain French general who broadcast on the English radio (though in fact the Count's only objection to him was that his name had a "de" in it yet he in no way belonged to the nobility), Alphonse Burgaud had thought it wiser to say nothing and to keep his own counsel.

And that was why, a few weeks later, the Count was surprised to come across a strange-looking cowherd on his land, a cowherd sporting a tight jacket and black corduroy trousers much too short for someone of his height, trying to keep his feet in his wooden shoes as he walked with the herd, an open book in his left hand, which from time to time he stopped reading to give a lazy cow a little tap on the rump with his switch. For the young man had accepted the farmers' generous offer on condition that he would be allowed to work for them as a simple farm laborer. He got up at dawn to do the milking, which he said is much more of a skilled job than it seems. It isn't enough to tug at the poor animal's udders, pretending to be a bellringer, if you want the jet of hissing, creamy milk to come gushing down in great bubbles against the metal sides of the pail, its warm steam misting up the milker's glasses as it descends. He had worked for a long time to master the alternate movement, right hand, left hand, the calculated pressure of the fingers, the thumb and forefinger ringed round the teat so as to function like a valve and contain the flow of the milk before expressing it. This apprenticeship, under the critical and amused eye of the farmer, had not been without the odd mishap. For it is a risky maneuver. When the animal realizes she's in the hands of a clumsy incompetent, she will manifest her displeasure by flicking her tail — usually far from clean — in the face of her torturer, unless she suddenly skips sideways and knocks him — and his pail with him — over backward into the manure. With his cheek flattened against the animal's flank, precariously balanced on the three-legged stool that was far too low for his height, it was difficult for him to accommodate his long legs on either side of her distended belly, so that as soon as he was allowed to do the milking on his own, he invented the idea of tying up the cow's tail and muffling his head in a jute sack, and didn't hesitate to adopt unorthodox positions, such as sitting side-saddle, to avoid a kick from a bad-tempered beast, a bluish memento of which he still bore on his tibia.

From the spring sowing to the autumn plowing, he followed the complete cycle of the work of the farm laborer. He harrowed, scythed, harvested, sheafed the corn, garnered, hoed, weeded, paid special attention to the few tobacco plants intended for domestic use, and even took to pipe smoking, which he didn't like because the smoke went cold in the stem. He wielded the fork and the spade, mucked out the cow shed, filled the wheelbarrow with straw for the animals' litters, chopped the wood, held the pig down firmly while the farmer slaughtered it, almost passed out at the sight of its spurting blood, asked no more than to be excused from stable duty and from looking after the two heavy cart horses after one of them nearly

amputated his finger while he was trying to put the bit
between its teeth. (Years later, linking this episode to the
memory of his father, he confessed that he would have
made a deplorable dragoon.) The rest of his time he spent in
being bored, reading, doing odd jobs, putting up shelves,
repairing the handle of a plow, and sometimes disappeared
for days on end when there wasn't enough work to make his
presence indispensable. On some evenings he got on his
bicycle and announced that he'd be back at dawn in time
for the milking, and in fact they found him at his post,
having barely taken the time to change his clothes, as if
nothing had happened. His behavior never gave his hosts
any clue to his secret activities, and anyway, rather than
look for complications, wasn't it simpler to imagine there
was a girl involved? After all, that was only natural at his
age, and for a virile young man this cloistered life was no
life at all. But he didn't give them the slightest hint, except
on one occasion, after he'd been away for several days,
when the farmer's wife who was sweeping out the yard saw
him return, throw himself off his bike, rush into his room,
and immediately start burning some papers in the fireplace
and later go and scatter the charred remains on the compost
heap. As it was getting close to noon, the only words he
spoke were to say he didn't want any lunch because he
wasn't hungry, and then he went up to his room. A little later,
the farmer's wife, worried that he's so silent, knocks on his
door to offer him a cup of so-called coffee, a revolting liquid
made from roasted barley, and, getting no answer, feels justi-
fied in going into his room, which is that of her son who's a
prisoner in Germany. She finds it empty, the window wide
open on the sounds of the summer and the green mass of the
trees, and is only half surprised because she knows he is in
the habit of climbing over the rail so as not to disturb them

when he comes back from his nocturnal expeditions; then she catches sight of him lying under a tree at the edge of the forest, his head in his folded arms, a cigarette burning itself out between his fingers.

It had depended on a mere nothing — lazy pedaling, an overlong detour, a few minutes trying to find the meeting place, but without that saving delay he would have been with his comrade Michel Christophe, who had been arrested almost under his very eyes, shoved into a car, driven to Nantes, tortured at the Kommandantur — headquarters — imprisoned, and then deported to Buchenwald. When he came back after the war was over he was so terribly thin — almost as if he had no skin covering his head and bones — that when his mother met him on the station platform she didn't want to throw her arms around her poor son's body for fear of reducing him to dust, as sometimes happens to mummies that are handled without due care when ancient tombs are opened. "Is it really you?" she asked, not to convince herself that it really was he — even mutilated or disfigured, how could she not recognize this part of herself? — but the way people marvel at the metamorphosis of someone they know well: Is it really you? — we didn't know you were capable of such an extraordinary feat: Is it really you? — walking that lethal high wire? And day after day she fed him like a child with purées and minced meat, respecting his silence. And when he began to regain his strength, when his gaze began to seem less remote, he started to tell her about the suffering of the body: hunger, lice, vermin, dysentery, cold, fever. But how was it possible to explain that particular kind of hunger to people who in return talked about their own hardships; to describe the kind of itching that made you scratch until you drew blood and nearly went mad to people who complained that

soap was a rare commodity and never lathered, or that kind
of cold to people who had shivered for four winters, or that
kind of fever to people who had piled blankets and eider-
downs on top of themselves? So he kept the rest to himself,
and it was only very much later that he confided to his
friend Joseph something he had witnessed and had been
tormenting him day and night ever since his return: five
hundred little gypsy children, aged between five and twelve,
had been executed by lethal injections, one after the other,
lying on a table unable to move while a pseudo-surgeon, a
lift attendant in civilian life, stuck a long needle into their
hearts, filling them with a yellowish poison that caused
instant death. And his friend Joseph, remembering how
slowly he had ridden his bicycle, and the stroke of luck by
which he had avoided sharing the same fate, refrained from
asking him whether he had been one of the men who had
held the little martyrs down by force.

On Sundays, at Alphonse's invitation, he often spent a good part of the day with the Burgauds, where there were always several guests. The tailor prided himself on being generous and hospitable. His intellectual curiosity had earned him the friendship of a theologian and a Dominican friar — from which friendships it might be deduced that he was assailed by metaphysical doubts — and allowed him to keep that of the companions of his apprentice years in Paris when, as poor young provincials, they used to chase all over the City of Light to take part in the claque in exchange for a seat at a concert. Two of these friends, a graduate of the Ecole Polytechnique and a journalist, who had later made their way in the world, still came to visit their humble friend, and even more frequently nowadays since life in occupied Paris had become really difficult. They would all, and others as well, in particular a Chinese student — no one could imagine how he had landed there — come together in the big house in Riancé. The tall young man had been reluctant to join in their animated conversations ever since Alphonse, without naming him, had put him on his guard: the tailor had reported that the Count had told him of his amazement at seeing a copy of Balzac's *Louis Lambert* on the bookshelf at the farm, and that he found it hard to believe that such a book was his farmers' bedtime reading. This incident had prompted the theologian to call attention to the volumes on the living room bookshelves that were banned, and even to attack some right-thinking bourgeois authors. "Not all Bordeaux is fit to read," he had declared, and this was enough to make you tremble, for if

Henri Bordeaux, that fervent advocate of the moral order, the faith, and the family, was to be consigned to the forbidden books department, about the only thing left was *The Imitation of Christ*. This warning implied a serious threat for the future life of the master of the house, but he consoled himself by leaning back voluptuously in his big patinated leather armchair and enjoying the Havana cigar brought by his journalist friend, the founder-editor of *La Revue des Tabacs*. For Alphonse Burgaud was so constituted that he wavered between the sacred and the profane, being capable of going on retreat for a week with the monks at the abbey of La Melleraye, sharing their Spartan meals, attending their services, but also of disappearing for several days on end without anyone ever discovering where or with whom — which was no doubt not quite so blameless. But in both cases the result more or less came to the same thing: it was always a way of escaping from the house.

His love of music bridged the gap between the two sides of this waverer. Alphonse had won a first prize for violin playing at the conservatory in Nantes, and he had even studied harmony and counterpoint at the one in Paris, so music played a big part in the lives of the Burgauds. One friend brought his flute, another his viola, a third his cello; it was all the same to Alphonse whether he sat down at the piano or took up his violin, and the evening continued to the strains of this improvised chamber orchestra whose sounds, in the summer, could be heard through the open window and provided an accompaniment to Riancé's nightly slumbers.

Claire Burgaud was somewhat less than enchanted by these meetings. Apart from the fact that she saw them as yet another way for her husband to exile himself, she admitted — perhaps as a reaction — that music got on her nerves.

And to make her point perfectly clear, on the day when Marthe was giving birth to her third child, irritated beyond measure that anyone could indulge in such a futile activity while her daughter was suffering the pains of parturition, she burst into the living room, snatched the flute from the lips of a salesman of ladies' lingerie whom Alphonse had made a special journey to fetch from the station at Ancenis, and broke it over her knee as if she were breaking a branch. She had then handed the two halves of the flute back to the unfortunate musician and announced, "It's a boy." These outbursts of hers were legendary. She boasted that she had used up two veils on her wedding day, having torn the first one when it got caught in a door she had just violently slammed. (It must be said in her defense that this event could certainly not have been the happiest in her life, as their marriage had been more or less arranged by their respective families.) Her abrupt manner had once even caused her to impale her hand on one of those spike things that people keep on their desks to stick their bills on, much as Pascal piled up his *Pensées*. At the same time it perforated the paper it went right through the palm of her hand, leaving the impatient woman with a brown spot like the ones old people have on their hands, and when she did get older you couldn't tell the difference. There was an underlying bitterness in the way she did everything in double-quick time, as if everything was a boring chore to be gotten rid of as quickly as possible. Even her declared aversion to music actually went back to a frustrated vocation. As a girl, she had spent hour after hour practicing, but her father had been so exasperated by the fact she didn't do anything else that he had taken his ax to her grand piano, and now all that remained of it was the little mahogany table in a corner of the living room.

*   *   *

This was how the tall young man made the acquaintance of Marthe's two younger sisters. Anne, the middle one, was discreet, graceful, with a long, delicate nose, as slender as a Tanagra figurine (the Burgaud girls were all small: Anne, the tallest, was barely five foot), and seemed to hold herself aloof from the turbulence of the household, remaining silent, embroidering, strumming on the piano, always ready to join her father in his workshop and help the seamstresses with their sewing and machining. Lucie, the youngest sister, was still adolescent, slightly plump, always lively, quick to flare up, and had immediately offered her services to take his letters to him at the farm. He watched her arriving on her bicycle, always at top speed, cutting through the forest, less to shorten the journey than to add spice to her secret mission, bumping over the cart tracks, crouched over her handlebars, and still out of breath when she handed him the envelopes that he glanced at rapidly, turning them over and over as he looked for the longed-for handwriting, and as he slid them into his pocket she could read the disappointment on his face. "The letters aren't getting through," she would say, to soften the blow and suggest a reason for this unbearable delay. He would nod sadly. "The war always gets the blame," he would reply, as a way of casting doubt on the selective delivery of the mail that allowed his aunt's letters through and merely kept back those from his beloved. Although he had never mentioned it in her presence, Lucie knew his story. She had even considered writing to that Emilienne herself, to get her to break the silence in which she had been keeping her unofficial fiancé. But from what she had managed to gather from Etienne — although she hadn't been able to glean all the facts — it rather looked as if the blond Milady had been acting out her role in real life. Had the rumor reached Joseph? One day he put his letters in his pocket without even looking at them.

By way of consolation, whenever she got a chance Lucie would smuggle a little treat among the books he asked her to bring him — a bar of chocolate, which, as he always liked to say, was his vice. For this kind thought he nicknamed her "Little Red Ridinghood." And since on that day the messenger happened to be wearing a blue-hooded cape, perhaps wanting to bear a closer resemblance to the young man's description, she blushed.

He had now exhausted both the possibilities of the Burgauds' library and the dividends of life in the open air. When the harvest was over, he announced he was going to leave. He offered to fill the gap Michel Christophe had left in his father's workshop. And that was how he came to be under the roof of an old apartment block, strengthening its framework, on September 16, 1943, when the siren reverberated over Nantes — the howling of a terrified animal that the inhabitants had learned to take in their stride. The alerts had been almost continuous for several weeks with no other damage than an enforced break of an hour or so. People immediately stopped whatever they were doing and rushed down into the shelters in the cellars buried deep under the old city. The stone vaults that had already withstood three or four centuries were once again pressed into service. The knowledge of the cathedral builders was considered more reliable than that of the most out-and-out modernists.

A smell of mold greets these people voluntarily burying themselves, crowding together in a free-for-all on the benches, playing an original variant of musical chairs, ex-soldiers and the disabled — who are often one and the same — brandishing cards adorned with their photos and demanding priority, thinking that their past exploits justify a moment of weakness. The people who make a point of standing up wish to vindicate them, and are not so much offering them their seats as teaching the others a lesson. Reclaimed from the banks of the river, the alluvial subsoil releases its excess moisture through the crumbly stone walls. The people who have to stand don't like to lean against them, oozing as they are, and here and there covered in saltpeter like a harbinger of what is about to take place above their heads. A naked lightbulb hanging on its wire communicates everyone's fears to everyone else. Some people prefer to stay in the half-light and keep to themselves what the lighted arena so crudely reveals. Eyes meet, avoid each other, establish a short-lived complicity, and look away just before any secrets are confided. The proximity of death is no excuse for any lack of decorum. Keeping their legs tightly together, the women pull down their summer dresses, which reveal their knees and have never been so abbreviated. There's something to be said for shortages, after all, when a saving on materials is also easy on the eye. One man, leaning forward and resting his elbows on his thighs, wouldn't exchange his seat for anything in the world. With an air of profound anguish, his eyelids half lowered, his field of vision takes in his neighbor's crossed legs. Yet this would be the right moment to put an arm around her trembling shoulders, to press her frightened hand with his as a comforting gesture, for their terror is sometimes so extreme that people's hair stands on end, or even turns white between the beginning and end of an alert.

They all wonder whether their neighbor's place might not be a better guarantee of survival than their own. Which way lies salvation? Over there, rather than here? On this side where the vault is low, or in the doorway? Which future victim's number has already come up in this funereal lottery? When specks of dust start falling off a vault and sprinkling a head, its owner gives a start, raises his eyes to check the origin of this micro-earthquake, and without a word goes and picks another place. Although there are plenty of candidates, no one takes his seat. The people on either side of it automatically move apart, leaving a kind of well between them that is presumably the prime target for the disaster, as if it were possible that that little space marked by a handful of chalky dust could encompass the entire accumulated ruins of the ancient residence of the dukes of Brittany.

A great many of the refugees have come from the nearby moviehouse, the Katorza, in the street of the same name, between the rue Scribe and the place Graslin, where they are showing *The Count of Monte Cristo* with that good-looking actor Pierre Blanchard in the title role: two hours of the implacable vengeance of a rancorous maniac who hasn't an ounce of pity in his makeup. After the first part of the program, which consists of a documentary and the newsreel (a loathsome voice trumpeting a victorious advance of the Axis forces and a shot of the Marshal kissing a little girl waiting to greet him with flowers as he gets off a train), and after the intermission, just as the credits are coming up on the screen, over and above the sudden music, or rather as if it were the amplification of a cancerous note, a long, crescendo lament that has nothing to do with the score brutally interruptes the projection, makes the lights come on again, and sends the cheated audience rushing toward the exit. Commenting on the event in the long, low vaulted cellar, someone says, "*Avez vous vu Monte Cristo?*" to which others reply with a knowing smile that "*Non, ils n'ont vu monter personne.*" Then the conversations tail off, and waiting takes over. The silence floats up and curves around the vaults, arches its back, and is only slightly perturbed by the quickly stifled sound of a child's sob.

"Joseph, aren't you coming down?" No, he prefers to stay where he is. He feels safer under the roof timbers than in an underground shelter at the mercy of a random check for identity papers and no possibility of escape. Then, if anything actually did happen, he has no wish to be buried alive — or for that matter to be buried dead, either — and what's more, under a false name. Who would claim the body of Joseph Vauclair, carpenter, born in Lorient? Who would weep for him? Anyway, there have already been plenty of alerts, but nothing has in fact ever happened. The bombers content themselves with flying over the town at a great height and save their lethal cargo to release over the industrial banks of the great river or a bridge upstream. One evening, when a pilot had been shot down and he was helping him to cross the Loire, he had watched this spectacular "son et lumière" show, the horizon churned up by great geysers of fire, the golden pointillist reflections of the machine guns glinting in the water, and, through the screen of the night, the sweeping searchlight beams scouring the darkness and planting a very ancient idea of evil in the illuminated eye of a cockpit. "All right, see you later then, Joseph, but do take care." With the flat of his hand, Joseph pats the piece of the framework they've been restoring. "Don't worry, Monsieur Christophe, this is good and solid."

No sooner has the sound of the carpenter's footsteps disappeared down the stairs than a rumble, like the sign of an impending storm, can be heard in the distance, it grows louder, swells inordinately until it has invaded the whole universe, and soon covers the whole town with a dome of thunder, a mighty, deafening, mechanical drone, which prompts the tall young man to hoist himself up through a skylight to the roof, where he lies down flat on the slates, his face turned up to the sky, a front seat to salute the noble action of the liberators bathing so high up there in the blue empyrean, well out of reach of the reprisals of the anti-aircraft batteries, by which everyone recognizes the non-chalance of the Americans, because the English pilots, perfect gentlemen, take every risk and dive-bomb in order to gain precision and to be sure not to miss their target. And there are so very many bombers that they cast a shadow over the setting sun on this late summer evening, they form a black, shifting, perforated cloud, suddenly connected to the earth by a curious Jacob's ladder, its rungs crazily disin-tegrating as the bombs come tumbling down, whistling, from the open bomb bays, letting all hell loose as they crash on the ground near the rond-point de Vannes, their explo-sive chain advancing toward the place Bretagne, sending a series of columns of black flames swirling up and swelling above the roofs, which are perforated like cardboard boxes, now reaching the place du Pont-Sauvetout, so close that a conflagration hurls the observer up against a chimney stack, which thereby loses its cowls but nevertheless stops him from toppling over into the void, so the daredevil hastily retreats back into the attic, bruised and with his shoulder half dislocated, descends the stairs hunched up with his hands cupped over his ears, this pathetic gesture being all he now has to protect himself from the terrifying din, and it's useless to shut his eyes to try to lose himself in the contemplation of that star-spangled retinal darkness, with every detonation his body feels the vibrations of the ground and the walls, but he hangs on to the strange idea that he can't die under a false name, although he is still reluctant to go to the shelter the carpenter has told him about, under the Café Molière, just a stone's throw from the Katorza, but it's too late now, the tragic work of the plow is eviscerating the place Graslin, sowing murderous seeds that come as a total surprise to the incredulous passersby, who are like the villagers who heard the little shepherd boy cry wolf so often that they refused to believe him, up till then the alert had merely been a convenient excuse to leave their office, shop, or factory and saunter over to the shelters, but now they're rushing around madly in every direction, crying babes in arms whose faces are distorted by terror, with toddlers in tow, these in their turn trailing a toy or a teddy bear, swerving to avoid bombs and craters, knocked over by a shock wave, picking themselves up, starting to run again, putting off until later the thought of worrying about the trickle of blood coming from one of their temples, and on all sides there are shouts, exhortations to keep together, officials yelling out the names of the shelters, one explosion follows another, thousands of bombs fall on Nantes that afternoon, in the midst of which flares shoot up from the huge gashes in the pavement, severed gas pipes transformed into flame-throwers, as if the underworld inferno were joining its malevolent forces with the celestial wrath, and the heat is so intense around the Pharmacie de Paris, all its five floors ablaze, that the silver dishes in a nearby jeweler's are reduced to a mercurial sauce, yawning gaps appear along the building line where apartment blocks have been reduced to rubble, sections of walls slowly begin to wobble and then collapse in an avalanche of stones that close the streets, redrawing the plan of the town, and, together with the torn-up cable car lines, the girders, the skeletons of cars and the bits of mangled furniture, forming pathetic barricades against the insurrection of the heavens,

the buildings open up like dollhouses, with their beds al-
fresco, their fallen chimneys jammed up against a gable,
their wall lamps going into a nosedive but restrained by an
electric wire, wallpaper suddenly laid bare, as immodest as
women's underwear, the miracle of an unbroken mirror
hanging over the void, and already, under the piles of
stones, crushed, mutilated corpses, both of human beings
and of cab horses imprisoned in their shafts, heartrending
cries calling for improbable help drowned in the colossal
din, and outside the Katorza, in a cloud of dust and smoke,
wild-eyed, terrorized, the middle Burgaud daughter, the
frail Anne, the pretty Anne, who — and this is a first — has
cut her Thursday lesson to go to the three o'clock performance with her cousin, and she relates that without Freddy
she would have died on that September 16, 1943, bombed or
killed by shrapnel, but she would have died at twenty-one,
an incredible punishment for having preferred the beautiful, vengeful eyes of Pierre Blanchard to her accounting
lesson — oh Mother, keep close to your cousin, he lives in
Nantes and knows the shelters, don't stay there petrified on
the pavement in the middle of that deluge of stones of fire,
you must be very much alive and still as beautiful, when you
seal a love pact — and it will be quite soon now — with the
tall young man you were hoping for who is gambling his life
in the neighborhood, your eyes have already met on those
Sundays he spends with your family, you have detected an
underlying sadness, whose cause you can guess, in his gentle
smile, you have enjoyed his conversation — he has read a
lot and he knows thousands of things. You may even have
noticed that for some time now he has been trying to attract
your attention by a friendly word, by his considerate behavior, but you must admit that — like everyone else,
actually — you are susceptible to his charm, his high spirits,

his kindness, you have observed his good manners — and for you, they count — his natural elegance, his way of holding his cigarette between the tips of his yellow, nicotine-stained fingers, or of inclining his tall frame when he's shaking your hand to say good-bye, obliging you to look up at him, but it's common knowledge that tall men often marry short women, you've seen him, so skilled with his hands, repairing the doll of a little girl who has been evacuated to Riancé with her mother and handing back to the overjoyed child that miracle of plastic surgery, its eyes back in its orbits, its arm mended. You are not unaware that he has evaded forced labor and has been hiding at a farm in the vicinity — he'll be going back there for a few days for the autumn plowing — but don't go jumping to any hasty conclusions because we're talking about a brave man — do you know his nickname in the Resistance? Jo the tough guy, yes, you've certainly heard it, but he won't boast about it, it will come to light in a letter written at the end of the war by the head of the Neptune network, which he belonged to for a time, testifying to the fact that he carried out several dangerous missions and that his conduct and courage were always deserving of the highest praise, but he can't put up with any authority for very long, that's a trait of his character, you'll have to get used to it. And he changes groups the way he will later change employers, the next network is called Vengeance — rather a grandiloquent name, but you can understand — and after that we find him as an agent in the Intelligence Service, a volunteer liaison officer with General Patton's army, and incidentally it was then that he performed a most heroic feat of arms (and of love) in diverting the American convoy he was supposed to be guiding so that it passed through Riancé — to kiss whom, do you suppose? And then there's the famous episode of the motorbike later described by Etienne, with the Allies making their way toward Paris and the eastern frontiers, not bothering about the remains of the German army, which, cut off from its bases, has entrenched itself aggressively in what are later called pockets, and the one near Saint-Nazaire, which includes Random, is one of the most formidable as it won't surrender until the day after the Armistice, but the tall young man who has taken part in the liberation of his sector is not aware of this situation and is making a beeline for his family perched on the motorbike behind Etienne, whose head is eight inches below his, his inevitable beret pulled down to his ears, both of them drunk with the wind and their newfound liberty, which they celebrate in their own fashion as they speed through the villages hooting and zigzagging all over the road without rhyme or reason, and then at the bottom of the hill leading up to Random there's a German roadblock, he grabs his two pistols, one in each hand, preparing for them to force their way through, "Joseph, you're crazy," yells Etienne, who prefers stratagem and slows down as if he is going to comply but then abruptly steps on the gas, bullets come whistling all around them as, bent low over their machine, they suddenly plunge down a steep path on the side of the road, abandon the bike in a bog — the next day Etienne will innocently report that it's been stolen — but this time also our tall, brave young man gets away with it, and you too, Anne, you have the best reasons in the world to take great care of yourself, for yourself, for him, for us, so as not to die before someone has said a few words about us, we aren't important enough for anyone else to take on the job, we're too humble, too hardworking, and if you die on this dark day, what becomes of us? who will project us into the light? will you leave us, poor little things of naught, in the antechamber of life's

Translator's Notes

9 *Carte du Tendre*. The region of the tender sentiments, as mapped out by Mlle de Scudéry and members of her salon in the era of Louis XIV; she introduced it into her novel *Clélie*.

17 Pont-Aven. A small town southeast of Concarneau on the south Breton coast, where the river Aven opens out into a tidal estuary. Here an innovative school of painting acquired prominence in the last decade of the nineteenth century; its leading light was Paul Gauguin.

22 Médor. Roughly the equivalent of "Rover" for us; apparently comes from Medoro, the faithful Moor lover of Angelica, in Ariosto's poem *Orlando Furioso* (1532).

29 Ys. A legendary city buried on the seabed off Finistère. The city had stood by the water's edge, protected by a dike. Now the dike included floodgates to which none but the king held the key, but one night the king's daughter stole the key when her father was asleep and opened these gates, leaving the city — and her own lover — engulfed. On certain clear mornings, so the legend tells, the cathedral can be seen breaking the surface of the water. The legend inspired Lalo's opera *Le Roi d'Ys* and Debussy's piano prelude *La Cathédrale Engloutie*.

32 Procopius. Early sixth-century Byzantine historian. His work includes an account of wars waged by the Emperor Justinian the Great against the Ostrogoths and Vandals.

35 Anne of Brittany. Anne (1477–1514) inherited the dukedom of Brittany at the age of twelve and later defended its independence. In 1491 she married Charles VIII of France. He died in 1498, and in the next year she married Louis XII. This marriage "confirmed the union of Brittany and France," although the region was only finally incorporated into France in 1532 by François I, Anne's son-in-law.

38 Jeanne Hachette. Fifteenth-century heroine who was in the forefront of the defense of Beauvais when it was under siege by Charles the Bold. Her weapon was an axe.

38 Sully. Maximilien de Béthune, Duc de Sully (1559–1641), Superintendant of Finance under Henri IV, decreased taxation and reformed the corrupt system of collection. He declared that "Plowing and grazing are the two breasts of France."

38 The Battle of Fontenoy. Fought in 1745 near Tournai in Belgium during the War of the Austrian Succession, by the English and Dutch under the Duke of Cumberland against the Franco-Irish forces commanded by Marshal Saxe. At a crucial moment "the English officers saluted and called out to the French, 'Fire, gentlemen!' 'No, Sir, after you!' replied Count d'Auteroche (following Marshal Saxe's orders)." So the English did fire first, but they nevertheless lost the battle.

38 The Bridge of Arcola. Located in Italy, province of Verona, on the river Alpone. After a difficult victory over the Austrians, Napoleon, flag in hand, led the assault on the Bridge of Arcola on November 15, 1796.

38 The Duke of Aumale. The fourth son of Louis-Philippe, he served as an officer in Algeria and was involved in the abduction of Abd-el-Kader's retinue, May 1843.

38 Léon Gambetta (1838–1882). One of the founders of the Third Republic, and prime minister 1881–1882. During the Franco-Prussian War he organized the Resistance, escaping from Paris by balloon in October 1870 when the capital fell to the enemy, and continuing the fight from Tours.

40 "*Les Trente Glorieuses.*" Every French person can tell you what "Les Trois Glorieuses" are — the three days' fighting, July 27, 28, and 29, 1830, that culminated in the July Revolution — but I have found only one, Thierry Naudin, who knows what "Les Trente" are: "The term was coined by the economist-sociologist Jean Fourastié, based on 'Les Trois Glorieuses.' Les Trente Glorieuses refers to the 1945–1975 period of continuing economic growth in France when the country reconstructed itself, industry was modernized, and demographic expansion went hand in hand with considerable improvements in living standards."

42 The postman Cheval. Ferdinand Cheval, 1836–1924, the son of a peasant, started his working life as a baker's apprentice, then became an agricultural laborer, and in 1867 a postman, moving to Hauterives (Drôme) in 1869. On his thirty-three-kilometer rounds he began collecting stones; in 1879 he bought some land outside the village, and from then until 1912, with the stones he had gathered, he built the extraordinary edifice that came to be known as "Le Palais Idéal." (His spirit probably had something in common with that of Antonio Gaudí.) Le Palais Idéal was classified as a historic monument by André Malraux in 1969, and now receives on average 120,000 visitors a year. In February 1994 it was announced that the local Hauterives council was to buy the postman Cheval's monument from his descendants for 7.5 million francs.

43 André Le Nôtre (1613–1700). The gardens designed by this man (who was also an engineer and town planner) include those of Versailles and, in London, St. James's Park, Kensington Gardens, and Greenwich Park.

51 *Tres de mayo*. A day of executions in Madrid in 1808, during the Peninsular War. Goya commemorated it in 1814 with his paintings of both *The Second of May 1808* and *The Third of May 1808*.

65 *grande gueule*. A big mouth or show-off.

67 Vaux-le-Vicomte. Castle built between 1656 and 1659 for Louis XIV's unscrupulous treasurer Fouquet, who didn't enjoy it for long because from 1661 the last nineteen years of his life were spent in prison. The park is considered one of Le Nôtre's most perfect creations.

76 Le Cirque de Gavarnie. Said to be the most beautiful amphitheater in the Pyrenees.

76 Bertrand du Guesclin (?1315–1380, born near Dinan). Man of war, from a noble but poor family, who served the kings of France and made a good job of chasing the English out of various regions. A popular hero, his legendary exploits are celebrated in poems and songs.

81 Baron Gros. Antoine Gros, 1771–1835, was a student of Jacques-Louis David. His 1799 painting of Napoleon crossing the Bridge of Arcola (now in the Louvre) is familiar to every French schoolchild.

100 *Les Mystères de Paris*. Written in 1842–1843 by Eugène Sue.

101 *les fusillés de Châteaubriant.* Châteaubriant, northeast of Nantes, is
     a small town where the German army of occupation set up a camp
     for French political prisoners. Following the assassination of a
     high-ranking German officer, twenty-seven of these prisoners
     were shot as hostages on October 22, 1941.

104 *"Tiens voilá du boudin."* Rallying call used by the French Foreign
     Legion on any and every occasion. Here, the implication is that the
     enemy are slyly being referred to as German sausages.

104 Richelieu's cats. Cardinal Richelieu (1585–1642) liked to surround
     himself with a lot of cats.

121 Captain Charcot. Jean Baptiste Etienne Auguste Charcot, 1867–
     1936, was a scientist and explorer who commanded the French
     Antarctic expeditions of 1903–1905 and 1908–1910, the latter in
     the *Pourquoi-Pas,* "one of the best fitted out and most up-to-date
     vessels that ever put out on such a quest." Nevertheless, in 1936 it
     broke up on the reefs inside a fjord in Greenland, and Charcot and
     all but one of his crew perished. (Jean B. E. A. Charcot was the son
     of Jean Martin Charcot, the doctor who made discoveries in
     pathology, hysteria, hypnosis, etc., and taught Freud.)

123 Judex. A character in early twentieth-century popular detective
     fiction who kept popping up here and there when least expected (a
     bit like Fantômas and Zorro). *Judex* was written in 1917 by Arthur
     Berhède (1871–1937), but the character achieved fame through
     the series of films made by Louis Feuillade (1874–1925). "Feuil-
     lade's film series on Judex is listed as one of the major movie events
     of 1917" (Thierry Naudin).

141 *"Avez-vous vu* Monte Cristo? . . ."* One of the corniest old French
     puns, and, like most puns, untranslatable; a play on the film title,
     Monte Cristo, and the identical-sounding verb, *monter,* 'to go up.'